THE STORY OF A BLOODLINE

BOOK-1 OF 'THE FAMILY DRAMA' SERIES

BHARATH BOBBA

Thank you: Bobba Sreenivasa Rao, Bobba Sindhu Chowdary, Bobba Siri Chandana, Bobba Sree Jyothi.

I always wanted to write a Family Drama and that dream of mine wouldn't have come true if not because of the memories that you people gave me.

I will forever be grateful for your hospitality and kind nature.

• • •

Contents

Contents

Acknowledgements

I can never imagine writing this book without the help of-

My Beloved Readers that spent their valuable time in buying copies of my previous books & giving me the feedback.

Old School & College Friends: Nikhil Rayala, Pinaka Pani, Sai Nagendra, S Nikhil, HariBabu, Ashok Reddy K, Manikanta Chowdary, Harsha Narasimha Varma alias Kick Butowski, Harsha Lagudu, Sriram Meda, Leela Sai Kiran, Sai Ram Chandra Raju, Raghavendra Varma alias Bahubali, Sanath, Nithin, Bharath Ponnapalli, Ajith Vamsi, Roshan.

Old College Batch Mates: Chandra Harsha G alias The Handsome Hunk, Balaji Kurapati alias Steel Factory, Dinesh Chitturi alias Current Pole, Eshwar Peddi, Swaroop Gandem, K.R.K Sai Ganesh.

The Seven Pillars: Phani Varma S, Mahesh, Sai Chaitanya, Suraj Naidu, Akhil Venkat, Preetham Reddy, Gemini Ganeshan alias Rahul Sai Ganesh.

One & Only Loving Bestiee: Thanks for not being tired of my drama and Thanks for being my support system, always.

Online Friends & Family: Haarika, Venkatesh Patnala, Sahithi alias Saahi, rose_giyanna, Jayashree.

Intercontinental Family:
Timilehin Raphel alias BTS from South Africa,
Marleen from Netherlands,
Melissa from Netherlands,
Ben from Tunis,
Cyril from Netherlands.

Engineering Classmates: Hemanth Chan, Sai Pradeep Dasari, Sesha Phani G, Rajesh Kandula, Sanjay(the one great personality that travelled with me to the publishing office before I published my first novel), Lakshman Chitturi, Jagadeeshwar Reddy Mallela, Bhanu Prasad Nallapaneni, Priya Chowdary, Sushma, HariSai V, Sathya Siva Reddy, Vishnu S, Anudeep Chowdary, Aadhi Chowdary, Somu, HariKrishna.

Ram Mohan Bobba, Pooja Sri Bobba, Raviteja Alluri, SunilBabu Bobba, Likitha Cherukuri, Sravani Chinnamsetty, Siri Chowdary Bobba, Sindhu Chowdary Bobba, Pratyusha Bobba, Supriya Bobba, Neeharika, Likitha, Nithin, Pavani Chowdary Pathuri, Sri Vathsava Chowdary, Mallik Anna & other family members.

Game Dev Batch: Krishna, Chandu, Vijay, Rajesh, Mythreya, Lavanya, Swetha, Gopal, Kalyan, Praveen, Shiva. Thanks for all the good memories. Those days of smooth and the fun ride will never come back.

Special Thanks to: Sravani Chinnamsetty, Siri Chowdary Bobba, Lakshmi Bobba and Melissa.

Special Thanks to: Comrade a.k.a Viveka Sahasrani for helping me in overcoming the writer's block and also for the unending support. You are a gem, Comrade. Keep that fire burning in your methods and writings.

Special Thanks to: K.V.N Sir who taught me English in an utmost interactive way, Ruby Mam, Senthil Sir, Devi Mam, Deepa Mam & other faculties that encouraged me to write more.

Seriously, without the presence of all the above-mentioned people, at least one of the words would have gone missing from this book.

Sorry if I missed mentioning any names. I'm thankful to one & all that helped me in making it this far as a human & writer.

• • •

Prologue

It's like we all are present in a waterbody,

Our actions create ripples.

Those ripples effect the lives of others.

So, be careful with every word you speak and every move
you make.

• • •

The Definitions

Telugu: కుటుంబం అనగా ఒకే గృహంలో నివసించే కొంత మంది మానవుల సమూహం. వీరు సాధారణంగా పుట్టుకతో లేదా వివాహముతో సంబంధమున్నవారు. "కుటుంబం" అనే పదాన్ని మానవులకే కాకుండా ఇతర జంతు సమూహాలకు కూడా వాడుతారు. అనేక జంతుజాతులలో ఆడ, మగ జంతువులు వాటి పిల్లలు ఒక గుంపుగా సహజీవనం చేస్తుండడం గమనించవచ్చును. పెద్ద జంతువులు పిల్లజంతువులకు ఆహారం, రక్షణ కలిగించడం ఇలాంటి కుటుంబ వ్యవస్థలో మౌలికాంశంగా కనిపిస్తుంది.

English: Any group of people closely related by blood or marriage, as parents, children, uncles, aunts, and cousins are considered as a family.

Dutch: Familie is de groep personen waarmee men direct of indirect door middel van één of meer ouder- kind- relaties is verbonden. Maar het ligt niet altijd in de bloedlijn. Het kunnen ook mensen zijn die jou in hun leven willen. Mensen die jou accepteren zoals je bent en die willen dat je een gelukkig en tevreden mens bent.

Portuguese: Designa-se por família o conjunto de pessoas que possuem grau de parentesco ou laços afetivos e vivem na mesma casa formando um lar. Uma família tradicional é normalmente formada pelo pai e mãe, unidos por matrimônio, e por um ou mais filhos, compondo uma família nuclear ou elementar.

This is how the word "Family" is defined in different languages. No matter how these and the other languages define it, the bottom line is- It is a group of people that identify themselves as a group because of the blood or relation that they share with each other.

And also,
Family is yet to be defined as something that certain circumstances haven't shown us yet.

• • •

Family Tree

FINNIGANS
Charles
Anna
Frederick
Elsie
Donovan
Janet
Margaret
Francis
Catherine
Monika
Richard
Jack
Stella
Seth

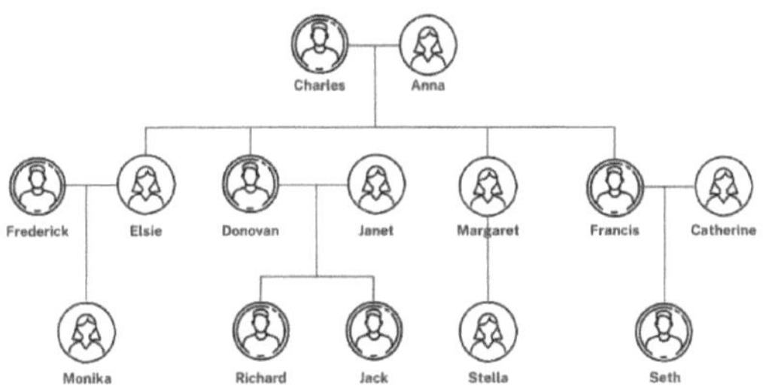

CHAPTER I

Jack Arrives

Jack woke up from a bad dream & found himself travelling back to his home after a long time. The voice in the back of his head kept on tormenting him by reminding him of the situations that led to this unplanned journey. In a rested posture, he sat there beside the window with cool breezes hitting his face, calm and lost in thoughts about his family members.

In order to reach Ferrierfield, Jack's hometown, one must travel to Tacro first & get into some other transportation medium that operates between towns and villages. When the green fields started fading and the buildings started appearing, he realised he was nearing Tacro.

"Dad, I'll reach Tacro in around 20 minutes. Will you be able to come & pick me up from there?" Jack asked his Father, Donovan over the phone.

"Is everything okay?" Donovan questioned Jack out of concern.

"Yes Dad. Everything is fine," Jack replied.

"I have some unfinished work at the farm. I'll inform Richard. He will pick you up from Tacro," Donovan said.

"Okay then," Jack said & hung the phone.

Richard arrived at the usual pickup point at Tacro on a motorcycle by the time Jack got off the bus with a handful of luggage.

"Is everything alright?" Richard asked Jack out of curiosity.

"Yes Brother," Jack answered while trying to enjoy the early morning countryside cool breeze.

Jack very well knew that this sudden & uninformed journey will surprise many, but he stayed calm, anyway.

By the time Jack reached home, his Grandparents- Charles & Anna were sitting on their porch, discussing something. When Richard & Jack were walking towards their house, Seth, Francis's son, the youngest one of the Charles's family, almost hit them ignorantly while chasing the hens belonging to the neighbouring house.

"How did you come, on a plane or what?" Anna questioned Jack.

"On a Bus," Jack replied.

"Then why haven't you informed anyone about it prior?" Anna asked Jack, pressing her tone.

"Did that cost you anything?" Jack questioned Anna out of frustration.

"No, why?" Anna replied.

"What's the purpose of this early morning interrogation?" Jack said.

"Come on in, Jack." Richard shouted in Jack's direction while holding the door open for him with one hand & the luggage in the other hand.

"Go on, have your breakfast, kid," Charles said while Anna continued murmuring something out of irritation.

As soon as Richard & Jack entered their house, Janet, their mother, served them breakfast. After the shower, he took a long nap for two and half hours & woke up all of a sudden when he dreamt of being pushed off of a cliff.

By the time Charles came back home from the farm & was sitting on the porch to exhaust the sweat, Jack came out sweating, stretching his hands.

"How's the journey?" Charles asked with his usual smile.

"Long & tiresome as usual. Got used to it anyway, Sir." Jack replied.

"Have you got used to the climate & the food there? Or are you still facing any difficulties?" Charles questioned Jack out of curiosity.

"At first, it used to be uncomfortable, but everything is fine now." Jack replied, smiling.

"Jack, when did you come?" Jack's first Aunt i.e., Charles's elder daughter, Elsie, asked him when she came there to call Charles & Anna for lunch.

"Earlier this morning," Jack replied.

"Can you please pass me over that vessel?" She asked Jack.

"Sure, by the way, where's Uncle Frederick? Haven't seen him since this morning." Jack asked Elsie out of surprise, for Frederick is almost always found sitting at home doing nothing.

She took a minute to make sure that Charles & Anna left for Lunch, then resumed-
"He went out on some work. So, how long is this vacation of yours gonna be?" She said in a different tone.

Even when that question made him feel not so nice, he took a deep breath & said "I don't know yet."

While they were having a casual talk, Donovan came back from the farm, drowned in sweat. On noticing Donovan's arrival, Elsie went back to the kitchen.

• • •

CHAPTER II

The Family Dining

2.1 The Family Dining Rules:

For the members of Charles's family to have a family dining, it will most probably be on one of the two occasions. One of it is in the case of some celebration like a birthday party or some other important occasion. The other reason when they'll sit together and eat is when the family is present as a whole, all the fourteen members.

Charles has laid some rules based on which this family dinner needs to be performed. Putting in a lot of thought and effort, he succeeded in getting a dining table designed out of pure rosewood based on his plan. The carpenters wondered how he thought of the model.

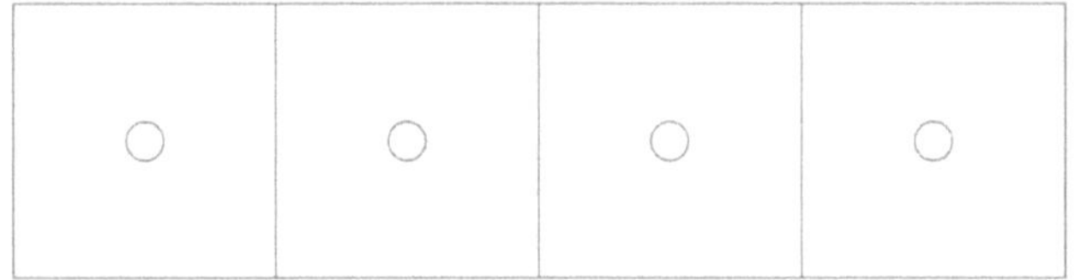

Top View

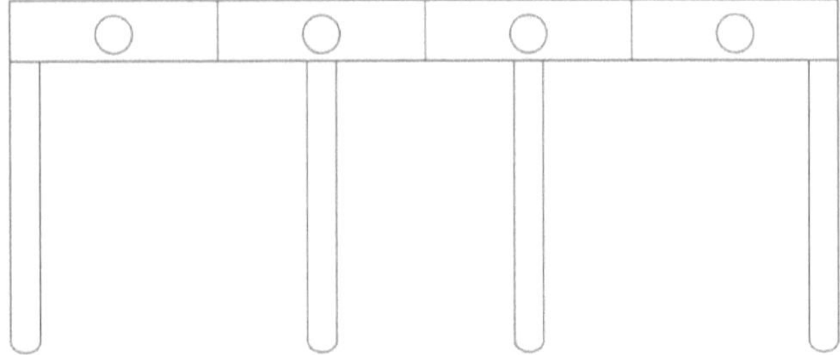

Side View

Their dining table design comprises of four individual tables that must be arranged one after the other and then held together tight with the help of three long sticks that have four medium-sized vertical sticks each, that will fit right into the holes made for them on the centre and on the two sides of the table. Charles got it designed in that way in order to make his children and their descendants understand that a family dinner can only be made possible by arranging the tables that he has given to their children during their wedding, one after the other and by holding them tight with those three long sticks that hold the tables at the centre and the other two sides together, by which he meant- they must share the affection and respect that will hold them together. He considered each of their children as the table parts and the long stick as the affection and the respect they must share.

Elsie, Donovan and Frederick received a table each. Charles kept the third part of the table and one long stick to himself. He distributed the other two long sticks to Elsie and Francis, which must be passed to and got back by the other two children of Charles. Elsie got rid of her stick by giving it to Donovan's house and never taking it back. Francis felt sad for Margaret since she did not receive the third part of the table that's meant for her, and he gave that stick to her permanently. But, whenever a family dinner is held, he used to go to Margaret's house and carry the stick, reducing that burden for her.

• • •

2.2 The Family Dining:

The family dinner starts by 8:00 PM only if the fourteen members of Charles's family are present there. Almost all the adults assemble there ten minutes before the dinner, but at least one kid shows up late. This time, it is Seth again.

When Seth arrived at the dinner setup panting, "What took you so long, Seth?" Anna questioned.

"It is the neighbouring hens again. They entered our premises, and I shooed them away. Let them come one more time. I'll nab some and use them in the cockfights." Seth said.

"Who's telling you about all this cock-fighting nonsense, Seth?" Anna questioned.

"My friends told me, you know what- I'm gonna place bets on those with the money you gave me. I'll buy you some chocolates if I win." Seth said mischievously.

In the next moment, Monika looked at Anna and asked her why she had never given her any money. Anna made a serious face, which made Monika immediately mind her own business.

A minute later, while everyone was having their dinner quietly, Seth said, "Mom, I have a question."

"Food first, questions later." Cathie said.

"Noooo Mom, answer my question. Listen, the question is- when Aunt Elsie, Uncle Donovan and Dad, got a table each, why didn't aunt Margaret get one?"

Cathie got stunned & failed to answer back. Instead, she gave Seth a look from which he must have understood that he's gonna be punished for that for sure.

When everyone else kept silent after that question, Charles cleared his throat & said-
"Seth, since Stella is a little girl, the chances are that- she might accidentally hit the one legged table and end up getting injured or breaking the table. So, I kept that part with myself. Now, have your dinner."

Besides Charles's words being utterly false, they didn't even seem to impact Margaret. She kept eating while also feeding Stella.

• • •

2.3 Post-Dinner:

Right after getting back home, Cathie caught hold of Seth's hand and warned him not to ask stupid questions at the dinner ever again.

*****

After the dinner, Donovan reached his home and kept hissing, "Lies, lies, lies all the way."

"Please stop it. Someone might hear you." Janet worriedly requested Donovan.

"What if I am? Does anyone even care? What did that poor girl do? At the end, is it her that is to be held accountable for how things have happened?" Donovan shouted.

"What happened Dad?
What Sir Charles has said out there, isn't it true?" Jack asked out of confusion.

Janet interrupted and brought an end to that discussion.

*****

"Have you seen her face when my father answered Seth's question? Not even a single muscle moved." Elsie said.

"Yeah, she kept eating as if she hadn't eaten in years." Frederick replied with a smirk.

*****

"Mom, will we get that table part when I grow up?" Stella asked Margaret.

"Yes, dear. You'll grow bigger by tomorrow only if you sleep now. Go to sleep." Margaret said, holding back a thousand unspoken things inside her.

"Okay Mom. Good Night." Stella said and slowly fell asleep.

'*Why would I even be alive if it wasn't for you, sweetheart? We will get the table. I will get it for you at least.*' Margaret said to herself.

• • •

CHAPTER III

The Details

The words that Donovan spoke the previous night made Jack realise that he didn't know his aunt at all. He likes her for her kindness. At the breakfast, he kept thinking about why he never attempted to get to know Margaret besides her attentive nature towards him and the other family members.

After breakfast, Jack headed towards Margaret and found Stella heading to their house.

"Good Morning Princess, had breakfast?" Jack questioned Stella.

Stella blushed and replied, "Yes brother, and you?"

"Yes, just now. Aunt Janet is inside, go." Jack said and left for Margaret's.

Jack found Margaret in her kitchen doing dishes. He asked her whether it is a good time to talk with her or not. Margaret welcomed him with a smile and said, "Yes, Jack, just regular work. By the way, I didn't get to speak with you yesterday. So, how are you?"

"I'm okay, aunt. What about you? How's your health?" Jack asked her.

"I'm good, dear. So, what do you want to talk about?" Margaret said.

"I don't know whether you'll be comfortable discussing yesterday's dinner or not. But I felt that we aren't reciprocating at least half of what you shower on us."

Margaret laughed a bit and asked Jack with a smiling face, "Why do you feel so?"

"I don't know whether everyone can see this or not, but I can clearly see from your actions that you care about your two brothers and your parents. In our family, you seem to be the only person who cares about most of the people here. But your brothers and parents only seem to care for you occasionally." Jack said.

"Hahha, so young and yet a lot of observation, huh?
See Jack, everyone will get busy with their lives. Leading those busy lives, some might forget to care about their family members, but that shouldn't make us do the same for them. Because, you won't be left with a family if you reciprocate ignorance." Margaret said.

"I still remember you feeding me lunch and dinner, no matter how busy you were back then. And as far as I know, I used to spend most of my time playing on your porch. For most of the time, you used to take care of me more than my mother. Besides knowing all these, my mother doesn't interact well with you & I don't understand that," Jack said confusedly.

Margaret took a minute and told Jack, "Your mother lost her parents at a very young age. Even before she forgot the affection that her actual parents had showered on her, she moved in and out of two foster homes & finally settled in the third. The foster parents of the third foster home are two sides of the same coin. They behaved rudely when they were inside the house and acted kindly when they were present outside the house. Poor Janet felt that this rudeness is the common nature of foster homes and the foster parents.

Instead of being treated as a child, she was forced to do all the household work, to which she got used to in no time. Even when she had the chance to complain & get shifted to some other foster home, she didn't do so, thinking that it'll be the same everywhere. Her foster mother hasn't allowed her to go out and play with neighbouring children of her age, thinking that she might speak out about the way she is being treated.

The situations that she faced as a child are cruel to the core. And those situations turned her into a cold one. She evolved as a kind human, but with caution. She is over-cautious about people that live around her. Even after coming into this family as the daughter-in-law of Charles, I did not see her demanding something. She was content with her husband and children. Although, she always felt that it would have been nice if she too had her parents. She seldom visited her relatives, that too when there's an occasion.

After getting married to Donovan and coming to Ferrierfield to live with Donovan, she observed that aunt

Elsie is far different from what she represents to the outside world. In most situations, Janet felt that Elsie is intentionally trying to prove that Janet is just lucky enough to land in the family of Charles and enjoy the riches, which obviously sounded like she doesn't deserve them. Janet hated that feeling. But she didn't take a chance to retaliate, out of the respect that she had for Charles and Anna. I occasionally overheard her sharing every little detail with your dad about the conversations that she had with Elsie, which made Donovan far more furious. Donovan didn't seem to be surprised though, maybe because he knew the real colour of Elsie right from his childhood.

For some reasons, Janet saw herself in little Stella, which is why she spent more time with her by adoring her. Stella found the kind side of Janet among the family filled with people of several kinds. Having seen the real colour of Elsie, Janet maintained distance from me too, thinking that I too might become the same proud & possessive girl of this home one day.

I clearly understood Janet's fear that stopped her from being nice & close with me. The presence of Janet made my daughter feel safe and comfortable. It made me happy. I look at Janet almost in a similar way that Janet looks at Stella.

Janet's treatment towards Stella also resulted in her (Stella) forming a great affectionate bond with you and Richard. I also know that both of you brothers (Jack and Richard) love spending time with your little sister."

"Thanks for explaining all these, aunt. My mother told me about her childhood, but it's like scattered bits. Now, you connected all the dots." Jack said.

"It's important to know about and care for our family members, Jack. So, you need not thank me." Margaret said with a smile.

"Aunt, as you know, I stayed in hostels most of the time. I dreamt of my family all the time & I thought I knew what it was. But, after coming here, I felt that this family of ours is far different from what I imagined till I came here. Do you mind telling me more about our family members?" Jack said.

"It is fine Jack. I'll help you connect all the dots." Margaret replied.

"Thank you, aunt. I'll come back here some other day. We can talk then." Jack said and left.

Margaret has never seen someone from this nuclear family that is as enthusiastic as Jack to get to know the family members. After explaining to Jack about his mother, Margaret felt some sort of relief.

• • •

CHAPTER IV

The Truth and A Part of It

Respect is a two-way thing. Wherever it is present, it must be taken as well as given. People like Elsie & her daughter, Monika, who is her close reflection, almost always took it, but never gave it back to anyone in real life. Being the eldest child in the family, Monika should have treated the youngest ones in the family with care & affection. All she ever cared about was her comfort & looks.

On many occasions, Jack tried to interact with Monika, hoping that she has an affectionate side to her ignorant behaviour. But she never really cared.

One incident that changed Jack in his childhood:
"Aunt, I don't know why, but this little fellow over here keeps strolling in the school corridors every now & then." Monika complained to Janet.

"Is it so, Jack?" Janet asked Jack seriously while combing his hair.

"No! Mother" Jack replied.

"Haven't I seen you strolling in the school corridors with a group of your friends today?"
Monika asked Jack.

"Ooooo Yess," Jack replied happily, remembering the fun he had that afternoon during the leisure hours.

Right in the next moment, Janet shifted the comb to the left hand, held Jack's hair firmly with her right hand & shrugged his head with great force. She even hit Jack several times with that comb. That sudden response from Janet shook Jack & it raised his fear levels. He literally begged her to let go of his hair.

"When did you become so reckless?
Are you even watching your tone?
All of this is because of those stupid friends of yours. They've spoiled you enough. If I ever see you with them again, you'll be seriously punished." Janet warned Jack, looking straight into his eyes.

Jack is purely out of luck that day. If Donovan or Richard were home when Monika complained about Jack, the punishment wouldn't have gone to such extreme length. Donovan would've scolded him and asked him to never do that again. And, Richard would've clearly explained to Donovan and Janet that Jack had strolled in the corridors along with his friends because of the leisure hours they got due to some ongoing decoration activities by their teachers for the next day's event.

By the time Donovan & Richard got back home from Tacro, Jack slept on the floor in the bedroom's corner, fully covered with sweat & tears. Donovan woke him up & when asked about why he slept on the floor, Jack narrated everything that happened in their absence. Richard explained why Jack & his friends did so. Donovan scolded Janet for being rude to Jack & requested Jack to have dinner.

Even as a child, Jack never tolerated injustice. He was brought up as an obedient kid & he always stayed honest. That day, Jack hated two things. One is Janet's unthoughtful action. Second one is Monika's revelation of only a part of the truth and not the entire truth. This made Jack hate her (Monika) for life. Richard felt irritated after seeing what Monika had done to his innocent little brother.

• • •

CHAPTER V

The Drama

07th June 2022:

Jack woke up by 7:00 in the morning and found Richard packing his luggage.

"If it's possible, stay for a few more days." Jack said to Richard.

"I'll come back again soon. Now I can't extend the leave anymore. The work is piling up day by day. I must go." Richard said.

"Next time, try staying for a week at least." Janet said to Richard.

"I cannot guarantee that, Mother. But, I'll try." Richard said.

"If you're done with your sleep, you need to drop me in Tacro." Richard said to Jack.

"Okay, I'll be ready in twenty minutes." Jack replied.

By the time Richard was leaving, Donovan was discussing some farm related work with Charles, while Charles was having his breakfast sitting on his porch. They both smiled at Richard while he was leaving, as a sign of wishing him a happy journey. Margaret and Stella stood on their porch while Stella waved Richard goodbye. Richard smiled at them and got on the motorcycle.

Jack and Richard reached Tacro in half an hour from Ferrierfield. Richard's workplace is a five hours' journey from Tacro. While Jack was carefully driving through the crowds of students that were just entering the college, Richard was telling him the directions for his bus pickup location.

While passing through St.Jones College (Monika studies there), something caught Richard's attention.

"Slow it down, Jack. Isn't it Monika there?" Richard said, pointing to a guy and a girl present in the empty area beside one of the sidewalls of St. Jones.

Jack verified that it's Monika. He also recognised the one that's evidently pleading Monika as Billy, one of his (Jack's) acquaintances during his schooling.

"Do you want me to drive there?" Jack asked Richard in confusion while observing Billy & Monika's ongoing discussion that seemed serious.

"This is not a good time. I won't be able to catch the bus if we don't reach the pickup point in five minutes. Drop me there and enquire your friend about their problem while going back home." Richard said.

After dropping Richard at the pickup point, Jack left from there immediately in order to meet Billy. Billy himself spotted Jack first and asked him to stop.

"Get on the bike, Bro." Jack said.

"Are you going out on some work?" Billy asked Jack.

"No Bro. I just dropped my brother at the bus pickup point and was going back home. In fact, I was looking for you to talk about you and Monika." Jack said.

"How did you get to know about us two?" Billy asked Jack out of surprise.

"I saw you two while I was going to drop my brother. You seemed worried. So, tell me, what happened?" Jack said to Billy.

"As you already know, I actively do my part in organising college events. A few months ago, one of my classmates introduced me to Monika, saying that she is also interested in organising college events. We have become good friends in no time. At some point of time, she slowly started getting friends with my crucial event management contacts throughout the college.
In the beginning, I was okay with it. Later, I got to know that she is also moving friendly with the guys that have got event management skills and ill intentions. I warned her to stay away from those guys. Besides ignoring my warnings, she went straight to those guys and told them what I told her about them. Those guys created a scene one day, provoking me and some of my guys to fight with them. With the help of some seniors, I settled the issue without letting it lead to a fight.

From that point, I understood her double masked nature and avoided her as much as possible. Unfortunately, by that time, she gained sympathy and support from half of my supporters. Then she started the actual drama. She approached my girlfriend and complained to her that I was troubling her (Monika) to love me. Unfortunately, my girlfriend believed her and started distancing herself from me. Most of my friends aren't trusting me anymore. Thus, in the process of helping Monika, I got trapped in complicated problems.

The worst part in this is- she got involved in her whole made-up story and is warning me that she's gonna lodge a harassment case against me. I don't know how, but she got some slap marks on her cheek yesterday & she's blaming me for that too.

You know me very well; I don't raise my hands on anyone, especially girls. You seem to be the only person who can help me in getting out of this situation." Billy said to Jack with tears held back in his eyes.

"When there's no fault of yours, why do you worry?
Why don't you tell your parents about this, if Monika really lodges a complaint against you?" Jack responded.

"There are two problems here, Jack.
First thing, the police won't believe me or consider me as innocent, given all her high level drama & those mysterious slap marks that appeared a day ago.
Second thing, my parents haven't been nice to each other for a long time. Within those closed doors and never-opened windows, my home already resembles a political war-room everyday. I don't want them to quarrel more because of me. I got used to the chaotic environment at

home, anyway. But I'm afraid that their words might lead to actions, which might create worse problems." Billy said to Jack.

"Billy, I trust you. If everything that you told me is true, I'll show up when it's needed and I'll help you in getting back your peace. You can trust me on this." Jack said and left from there.

• • •

CHAPTER VI

Knitting the Net: To Rescue One & To Trap the Other

After meeting Billy in Tacro, Jack went to meet one of his old friends that lives nearby St. Jones, in the lunch hours. Later in the evening, he went to meet two other close friends of his to discuss with them about the issue. While on the way back home, he just imagined explaining the situation to each of his family members and he visualised how each of them would react separately. Only Charles and Margaret seemed to be the workable options to be considered for solving this issue. The mindset of each generation of people differs, the older the generation - the lesser it understands about the current happenings. Hence, Jack felt that Margaret can understand the situation and provide him with some reasonable and mainly an implementable solution.

After getting back home, he directly went to meet Margaret while she was sitting on the porch and playing with Stella. He too played with Stella for a while and told Margaret that there's something important that he wants to discuss with her. Then, Margaret asked Stella to go over to Janet's and play there. He told her everything, beginning from what Billy has told him, to what he has learned from enquiring his three friends.

She thought about it for a while and said, "I think I can help you with this, Jack. Just give me an hour."

Jack left and went back to Margaret's in an hour and noticed that she's waiting for him in the hall area, holding a sealed envelope in her hands.

She handed it over to Jack and said, "Here it is, Jack. There's an old friend of mine named Henry. Hand it over to him. He lives right next to the Main Power Station in Tacro. His house is coloured light blue as far as I remember."

Jack travelled to Tacro right away to hand over that envelope to Henry. With the directions that Margaret had told him, he easily spotted Henry's house and handed him over the sealed envelope. Henry took a peek over the envelope and found "To: Henry, From: Margaret." written on it.

"My Aunt Margaret asked me to give it to you, Sir." Jack said to Henry.

"Thank you, kid. I'll look into it. Tell Margaret I said hello." Henry told Jack with a smile.

Then Jack went straight to Billy and dictated exactly what Margaret told him to say-
"Billy, all the necessary arrangements were made. If everything that you told me is true, you'll be saved for sure. I'd like to add something- If Monika ever dares to drag this whole cooked up story to the police station, then first plead her in order to make her pickup her pride & the moment she does that, break it off and let the whole scene go to the police station. Trust me, we got this."

"Okay Jack, thank you. Let's see what happens." Billy said in a worried tone.

"Don't thank me now, Bro. It's too early for it. You can thank me when it's all settled. Take Care. Here's my number. Call me in case of any emergency." Jack said with a smile and left.

• • •

CHAPTER VII

KARMA

Two days after the arrangements were made, Billy texted Jack, "Bro, it's good news. We must meet. Come over to my place in the evening, if it's possible." Jack felt relieved after reading Billy's message. While he sat relaxed on their porch, half an hour after he received Billy's message, Charles came home along with Frederick and Monika. Charles seemed serious, while the other two looked confused and frightened.

Charles failed to control his anger and started scolding Monika right in front of her father. Then he said, "Frederick, what were you doing when she even got slap marks on her face? Teach your daughter some manners. We will not always be able to help our children if they keep on committing mistakes without our knowledge."

"Sir, when asked about those slap marks, she told us that one of her female classmates hit her when they got into a fight about some project related issue. Elsie even warned her not to get into such fights again. But, anyway, I'll talk to her, Sir." Frederick said, making a pathetic as well as a disgusted face. He then dragged Monika into the house and told Elsie everything that had happened at the police station. Right after the moment that she got to know what her daughter has done, she thrashed her multiple times with Frederick's leather belt and said, "Can you explain your actions? Or do you want to get more beatings?"

"It's your drunkard husband that actually stole those old notes from Charles and asked me to exchange them for some greater value. He even used to drink with the money that I got in exchange for those old notes of Charles." Monika said, weeping.

"Why didn't you tell me when all of this is happening?" Elsie questioned Monika.

"Why should I tell you?
You never gave me any money when I asked you. This way, I at least used to get some money to buy whatever I like. So, I continued doing it." Monika said.

Elsie clearly saw her wrong-parenting after listening to Monika's rant. She also understood that Monika might crack up under some more pressure from her. So, she shifted her concentration on to Frederick and started thrashing him with his own belt, saying, "You already exhausted all our wealth by drinking that rotten alcohol for years and years, now you're keeping our daughter's neck in line. You deserve these beatings. Have some more."

"No, no. I'll never drink again. I'll never do that. Please stop this Elsie." Frederick begged her in pain.

Elsie threw that belt away and got back to her cleaning work, unable to face her daughter.

In the evening, Jack went to Billy's place. He invited Jack to his house. There they sat in Billy's room, where he narrated to Jack what actually happened at the police station.

"I cannot believe this, Bro. I mean, I wholeheartedly intended to help you. But I didn't think that Monika is this dumb of a person, having known what her mother is capable of." Jack said out of astonishment.

"Even I stood awestruck on seeing how the events took shape in the police station." Billy said.

"So, tell me the whole thing that happened after I left." Jack asked.

"To be honest, your words that night gave me some hope. Especially when you said that the arrangements were made. I cannot deny my insecure feeling though. Because it's your sister that we are going against. So, I was also a bit afraid." Billy said.

"Bro, I don't like calling her my sister or to be called as her brother. That's why I only call her by her name & never with the relation. In my childhood, she once made my mother beat me unnecessarily by saying the half truth. I would've let it go if that was unintentional. But, she did it intentionally, and she hasn't changed a bit. She has the sickness of enjoying children younger than her cry. Such a sadistic person she is. Her mother is a whole another level of weirdness. Her actions and words will be completely opposite, always. The reason that I wanted to help you is only because of your innocence. It has nothing to do with her being my family member." Jack said.

"Ohh, I'm sorry Bro. I didn't think that she was cruel towards her family members, too." Billy said.

"Anyway, it's not your fault. I'm excited to know what really happened after I last met you." Jack said.

"The night we met, a kind of gut feeling started developing in me. All these years, I lived a happy life with my friends within the college walls. The only reason that I enjoyed being in college is also because of not being present in this huge house filled with just people that regularly fight with each other and keep misunderstanding each other.

Till that day, I literally begged her not to complain about me. I know that I'm innocent and I need not be afraid of her false allegations. But she eventually turned my friends against me and made me feel guilty for everything that she cooked up on her own. And you are the only person with whom I've shared all of this with. After sharing that, I felt relieved of the burden that I have been carrying on my shoulders for so long.

Then I started ignoring her, which made her more egoistic. And this morning, I did like you told me- I made her pickup her pride and let that pride of her make her step into the police station. Right after walking into the police station, she rushed into the Chief's chamber, leaving me in the waiting area. While I overheard her requesting the Chief not to inform anything about this at her house, some other officer came towards me and asked me if it's the girl named Monika from Ferrierfield. I verified that she's Monika from Ferrierfield. The nameplate on that officer's uniform read Henry.

Then officer Henry went into the Chief's chamber and asked Monika to wait where I was standing. The Chief and officer Henry discussed something for around five minutes.

Officer Henry then came out and asked us to be seated. They asked us to narrate our versions. She blamed me and narrated her whole fabricated story to them. I said that I'm innocent, and that I had nothing to do with all that she's blaming me for. Then they made some calls. I didn't understand what was happening at that moment. Twenty minutes later, it all started making sense." Billy said and took a deep breath.

"What happened next?" Jack questioned Billy.

Billy exhaled with laughter and said, "People started coming then. People that were necessary in proving my innocence, people that were necessary in telling the truths behind her cooked up story, and finally the people that are capable of punishing her for her wicked acts."

"And who are those people?" Jack questioned.

"First came in our Drama Queen's truest and only friend, Rebecca. And maybe because of the whole police station environment, she vomited everything that she knew about Monika. It left me awestruck after listening to what she told the officers about Monika." Billy said.

"What did she say?" Jack questioned.

"She revealed that it's Monika's boyfriend that actually slapped her. Monika started speaking the truth then. She said that the name of her boyfriend is James. He is a drop-out of St. Jones. He can be seen on the college campus selling some nonsense stuff to the students. When questioned about how she met him, she confessed that he used to buy the old currency notes that she stole from your grandfather's old collections for a higher exchange.

Later, she found out that James is a rogue. It is only then that she intentionally got close to me. She even told James that she's in love with me (Billy) in order to get rid of her rogue boyfriend. Instead of leaving her, he got enraged and slapped her.

And by that time, when I felt that all of this was over, your grandfather came in along with your uncle, i.e., Monika's Father. Apparently, officer Henry informed him about this entire scene. And it looked like they both knew each other. Then your grandfather scolded her for all that she has done and asked her to apologise to me. She apologised. The officers wrapped it up without even asking me to inform or call my parents regarding this." Billy said.

"And how did Rebecca's face look when she left?" Jack asked Billy.

"She looked frustrated. But why are you asking that in particular?" Billy questioned.

"On the same day that you told me about all this, I went to meet three of my old friends. One of them suggested that I meet Rebecca, since she is Monika's closest friend.

Then I went directly to Rebecca's and tried speaking with her nicely. She showed off as expected. Then I threatened her to either speak up the truth or be summoned to the police station when this gets worse. I even lied to her that Monika is planning on throwing the blame on her when this issue gets serious. Then she confessed everything that she knew. She might not have expected that she would be summoned." Jack said.

"And how come does the Chief and officer Henry did all this to prove my innocence? I didn't get it." Billy said.

"Officer Henry is an old friend of my second aunt (Margaret). She decided to help you the moment I explained her everything that I found out from you and my friends about this issue." Jack answered while preparing to leave.

"Thank you so much, Jack. Also, thank your aunt on my behalf. I'm feeling alive after a lot of days." Billy said while bidding goodbye to Jack.

• • •

CHAPTER VIII

Letter to an Old Friend

The next afternoon, Jack went over to Margaret's and waited in the hall area after noticing that she was having her lunch.

"Come here Jack, have lunch," Margaret said.

"No Aunt. I already had mine half an hour ago." Jack answered while looking for Stella.

"Stella is sleeping. I don't know why, but she's sleeping unusually more these days." Margaret answered.

"Maybe someone might have told her that she might get dark circles under her eyes if she doesn't sleep more." Jack said, laughing.

"Hahha, she's too young to understand even what it means. Are you that someone or what?" Margaret said while walking into the hall area by finishing her lunch.

"No aunt. She's an obedient kid. Unlike Seth, she always responds with her smile and innocence." Jack said.

"Nice. By the way, how's your friend doing?" Margaret said.

"To be precise, he is feeling alive after a lot of days. He also asked me to thank you on his behalf." Jack said with a bright smile.

"I'm glad that we saved him from being affected by one of our family members. I cannot deny the mental suffering that he might have gone through till yesterday just because of Monika's behaviour. But we at least saved him from falling into worse problems." Margaret said in a tone of relief.

"But Aunt, I didn't understand what exactly happened. All these events rushed unbelievably, as if it was a dream. Will you tell me what that envelope contained?" Jack said.

"Your curiosity levels haven't dropped even a bit. In your childhood, you used to ask me a lot of questions about the sky, the stars, the moon and a lot others. You grew so fast, kid.

Okay, I'll tell you about that envelope. As I have already told you that day, Henry is an old friend of mine, mutual friend actually. We went to college together. He is a nice person. When you came to me after enquiring your three friends and that girl Rebecca, you sounded confident enough about Billy's innocence. The moment you mentioned Monika warning Billy that she'd approach the police, Henry came to my mind. Although you were uncertain about this issue going to the police, I very much wanted it to go there. Since we will surely be able to resolve the issue with the help of Henry there. Hence, I wrote a letter to Henry and placed it in the envelope that I asked you to give him."

• • •

The Letter:

Hey Henry,

This is Margaret. There's a problem. I need your help to solve it.

If my niece named Monika comes to the police station complaining that a guy named Billy is harassing her or might cause harm to her, please don't jump into any conclusions right away. First, call her best friend, Rebecca, to the station and make her speak the truth in order to find the reality behind Monika's allegations.

If Billy is found innocent, call my father and inform him about everything that happened there. Mention nothing about this letter.

This is just my attempt to help that kid, considering that he's innocent. Hoping that justice will be served. Burn this after you read it.

Your Old Friend,
Margaret.

*****

After the issue was solved, instead of burning it, Henry posted it to a stranger. And the stranger enjoyed reading each and every letter present in that letter.

• • •

CHAPTER IX

Jack & Stella

"So, are you planning on getting up anytime soon, or will you directly wake up for lunch?" Janet asked Jack.

"Anyway, I don't have any work to do, so what if I sleep for some more time?" Jack said.

"Getup, have breakfast and bring Stella here. She didn't come here for a week." Janet said.

Then Jack remembered Margaret's words, where she mentioned about Stella's recent unusual and excessive sleep. After breakfast, he went over to Margaret's and found Stella sitting alone in the hall area.

"What's the little princess doing?" he asked her.

"Nothing Brother." she replied in a dull tone.

"Where's Aunt?" he asked her.

"She fed me breakfast and went over to the neighbour's house to help them in some food preparation." She replied.

"Now, come with me. Let's go out and buy some chocolates." Jack said.

This time, even the word chocolates failed to bring the smile upon Stella's face.

"So, tell me what's really going on." Jack asked her.

She nodded her head as if there's nothing.

"Are you being this silent new person with me alone or with everyone else in the family?
When Richard was here last time, you spoke well with him. Now it seems like you don't enjoy talking with me. Is it so, Stella?" Jack asked her.

"No Brother, it is not about you. It is something else." Stella said.

"We are Family, Stella. Tell me. What's bothering you?" Jack asked.

While they were still walking back home, she started speaking.

"There is a group of students in my school. They come to school together and leave together. I tried getting friends with them, but they didn't seem comfortable." Stella said.

"Why is that so?" Jack asked.

"They're from an Orphanage. Right from the first day that they joined the school, most pupils looked at them differently." Stella said.

"In what way?" Jack questioned.

"They're considered as sad even when they're smiling and playing. Some others used to offer them pencils and chocolates even when they told them that they have enough of them. It is always like that. Others want to give them things and not ask them if they want to play with them." Stella said.

"It is Sympathy, Dear. People are sympathetic towards those that lost someone or something. But, in many cases, that sympathy will also be faked.
My advice for you is- you need not feel sympathy for them. But, you must treat them normally. If you ask them to come and play with you since they're orphans, it isn't correct. And the chances are that- they may not like it.
If you ask them to come and play with you since they're your schoolmates, it is completely fine. And the chances here are- they might come and play and also they might enjoy it." Jack said to Stella.

"Okay, Brother." Stella said.

"So, that's it?" Jack questioned.

"There's something else." Stella said.

"I'm your brother. Tell me what it is." Jack said.

"Last week, when I was playing in our yard, Grandmother Anna called me. She gave me some Cashew Nuts to eat and then she gave me a box and asked me to give it to Aunt Elsie. I went to give it to her. Aunt Elsie noticed that I was eating Cashew Nuts after seeing some of them in one of my hands. When asked about them, I told

her that Grandmother Anna gave me those. She took those leftover cashew nuts from my hand and asked me to leave. While I was coming out from Aunt Elsie's house, I heard her saying 'A girl that is brought from outside is being given those Cashew Nuts'. I don't know when these extravagant acts of my mother will come to an end.'
From that moment I was thinking that there is no difference between me at this house and those orphans at the school." She said and paused.

"Why do you feel like that?
Aunt Elsie behaves the same with all of us." Jack said.

"Only my Mother, Uncle Donovan, Francis, Aunt Janet, Richard and you treat me well. Why is that so, brother?
Sir Charles doesn't talk much with my mother or me. Why?" Stella questioned Jack.

She added, "And also, have you ever seen my father? Do you know anything about him? Some friends at school say that my father is dead, and that is why I cannot see him."

Stella's words literally shook Jack. Pretending as if Stella is exaggerating all these, he said, "Stella, you are unnecessarily imagining all these. If you say these to your mother, she'll get hurt. She cannot see you feeling sad. You know that very well. So, please stop misunderstanding all these situations. Those that aren't paying attention are just busy with their lives. Please remember and understand that we all love you very much."

Stella seemed as if she believed what Jack had said. Then he said, "Now come with me. Your Aunt Janet asked me to bring this Little Princess Home, since she forgot the way to our house from last week."

"Let's go brother." Stella said with a smile.

When Janet asked her why she didn't come to play there for a week. She perfectly lied that she wanted to sleep more. Later at lunch time, Margaret came and took Stella with her to feed her. Jack failed to stop thinking about what Stella said. Even he doesn't know whether Stella is really Margaret's daughter or if she is adopted. All he knows is bits and pieces, since Donovan and Janet never spoke about it fully in front of Richard or Jack.

That night, Jack failed to sleep well, for Stella's words kept roaming restlessly in his mind. Later that night, when he tried going back to sleep, he realised that he took his little sister's pain to heart. It kept him awake all throughout the night.

• • •

CHAPTER X

An Accident

One fine morning, after breakfast, Jack went over to Charles's and sat on their porch. Jack loves spending time in speaking with Charles, since he is the wisest one in the family. Charles explained to Jack how Ferrierfield has transformed in the last two decades.

After discussing for a while, while they both were at pause and enjoying the breeze, Jack received a mail on his phone from a person named "h.finnigan". Charles observed Jack smiling by looking at his phone.

"What happened?" Charles asked Jack with a curious smile.

"As I have told you once, I'm in contact with Finnigans from different states. I communicate with most of them frequently through mail.

Last month, in an attempt to send a mail to a person with the ID 'j.finnigan', I mistyped it as 'h.finnigan'. Seems like it is the ID of a woman named Hershel Finnigan. She mailed me that I sent the mail to the wrong address." Jack said, looking at that mail.

"What did you write in the first mail?" Charles asked Jack.

"I'll inform her that my last mail came by 'An Accident' to her." Jack answered.

• • •

Letter to Hershel:

Hello Mrs. Hershel,

Sorry for the last email. I mistyped the letter 'J' before Finnigan, and that is how it landed directly in your inbox. I usually communicate and build relations with Finnigans across different states by sending them mails and keeping in touch with them. And in an attempt to know the reason behind the long silence of a person named 'j.finnigan', I mistyped the mail address in a hurry. I was busy over the last month, so I failed to check whether I have sent the mail to the correct address or not.

Thank You,

Yours Truly,
Jack Finnigan.

• • •

"Done. I mailed her. Sir, have you ever met any Finnigans in other villages or cities?" Jack asked Charles.

"Yes. I met a few in some places that I worked in earlier." Charles said.

"Where do your parents come from? I have never seen them." Jack said to Charles.

In response to Jack's question, Charles sat in the resting posture, got lost in a deep thought and said, "I was born to the couple named Bancroft and Marie. I'm the second child in my family. My father is a low-wage worker who mostly worked in farmlands. My mother used to take care of the household work. One after the other, they gave birth to six children, all boys.

My father's hard work and my mother's efficient expenditure helped them to stay self-sufficient all throughout the way. While my elder brother and I attended school, my younger brothers haven't shown much interest in education. Instead, they helped my father with agricultural activities. My elder brother ran away from home during the schooling. In the end, only I entered and finished college.

After finishing the studies, I applied for a lot of full-time jobs and finally got the position of an Assistant Postmaster in a nearby village. Since the postal system is purely a government organisation, it consisted of frequent transfers between villages and towns. So, I travelled a lot during the initial years of work. Later, when I was promoted to the position of postmaster, the transfer process has finally slowed down.

Usually, those that are working as the Post Masters will be transferred to the areas within the smallest radius from the one that they previously worked in. But, for some reasons, I requested and got transferred to this Ferrierfield which is far away from where I worked all those years. My younger brothers stayed in our hometown (birth place), where they settled as farmers with the help of hard work and some inheritance.

I got married to Anna on 12th October 1946. I bought a small piece of agricultural and household land in Ferrierfield from my savings and with the share of inheritance. By the time I arrived here in Ferrierfield with Anna to settle here, we had our first child, i.e., Aunt Elsie with us. Since Ferrierfield is far away from my native place, my younger brothers failed to come and visit us in person. Instead, they wished us on our first child's birth through letters. After settling in Ferrierfield, we gave birth to your father, Aunt Margaret, and Uncle Francis.

So, that's pretty much it, kid."

From what Charles has told Jack, Jack had a few questions in his mind. But Charles seemed troubled when sharing about his elder brother and moving to Ferrierfield, so Jack kept quiet. He just smiled at Charles and then left for his house after some time.

• • •

45

CHAPTER XI

The Little Chaos

Anna likes her grandsons more than her granddaughters. One day, Jack and Seth sat in Charles's house watching TV. Jack went to the kitchen and brought some Cashew Nuts to eat. Elsie observed this from a farther distance.

On seeing Jack eating Cashew Nuts, Seth said, "I too want them."

Jack handed him a few and said, "Those are the only ones left from what I have brought."

"I want more," Seth cried loud.

"I got them from the kitchen, go and get them from there if you want." Jack told Seth.

"Okay, I'm gonna get those." Seth said, while running into the kitchen.

Seth returned scratching his head, saying, "I didn't find them."

Jack told him the exact spot & asked him to search there. Seth went into the kitchen again and started screaming that he didn't find them this time too. Anna went into the kitchen and started searching for them. Seth came back to watch the TV, hoping that Anna would bring them for him. Jack heard Elsie telling Anna that she kept them somewhere else and asking her to stop distributing those Cashew Nuts to the children in the family. Jack felt disgusted after hearing Elsie's whispers with Anna, for they weren't bought by her.

Anna returned empty-handed. She observed the irritation on Seth's face. So, she summoned Elsie & asked her to give Seth something to eat.

Elsie brought him three bananas that were a bit spoiled in some areas, on seeing which Seth's frustration went out of bounds. He immediately threw those three in the direction of Elsie and said, "They suck. I don't want them."

Two out of those bananas hit Elsie's face directly. She failed to withstand her anger and rushed towards Seth as if she wanted to beat him. She just thought of threatening him. On seeing her rush towards him at that pace, Seth jumped out of the chair suddenly and picked up a run. On seeing him slipping away at that pace, she actually started chasing him by picking a stick in the way. Seth fell down, hitting 'The Maple' with his leg and got his right hand fractured.

"SHE BROKE MY HANDDDDDDD. YOU DEVILLLLLL." Seth yelled. On hearing that, all the family members came out of their houses.

Catherine worriedly ran towards him and tried helping him stand by grabbing his right hand. Then he started screaming again in pain. Monika stood in a corner and laughed loudly because Seth's screams at that moment sounded to her like the squeaking while he struggled to get up from there. On seeing Monika laugh, Catherine threw one of her sandals at Monika in a rage. It missed hitting Monika anyway.

Everyone's looks immediately fell on Elsie next. She even had a stick in her hand, which she never intended to use. She just wanted to scare him away with that. Catherine yelled at Elsie for a continuous five minutes, without even giving her the chance to speak. During this heated situation, Seth told Catherine that Elsie had pushed him, adding fuel to the fire. Anna witnessed Elsie's hand reaching Seth's back while he was running, where her actual intention was to grab him by his shirt. While running, afraid of getting caught by Elsie, Seth kept looking back & front while running, and it was only then that he fell down by hitting the tree. Anna remained mute since she failed to decide whether or not Elsie had really pushed him. Elsie left with tears and a blown up face filled with disgust and powerlessness. Neither Charles, nor Donovan or Francis were present there when this incident took place.

A foolish person's rage shuts down her thinking capacity & only lets her see her prey & tells her to hunt it down. This is the same thing that made Elsie behave the way she did with Seth.

A mother's pain on seeing her child hurt doesn't let her think or see anything other than the one that caused that hurt. This is the same thing that happened to Catherine on seeing Seth hurt.

• • •

CHAPTER XII

The Scariest Childhood Memory

Francis got back home in the evening, Catherine told him everything that happened that morning by showing the Bandaged hand of Seth. Francis's reaction to that was not up to the mark of Catherine's expectation. Right from the beginning, she observed Francis's avoiding behaviour in Elsie's matter. This time, she lost her patience and picked up a fight with Francis, for it is her own son that is hurt this time.

"Cathie, please stop yelling and listen. You're acting in rage and pain. I'm acting out of experience. There's a difference." Francis said in a calm tone.

"What the hell! Francis, I have been observing you since our marriage. Whenever Elsie's matter comes up, you hide yourself like a tortoise hides itself in its shell. You aren't even afraid of doing something that's against the rules of your father. But what's making you avoid going against Elsie at all costs?
Is it because she's your elder sister?" Catherine said.

"It isn't because she is my elder sister.
It is because I know her more than everyone else that's present here." Francis said.

"Explain it to me. I'll decide whether your reaction in her case is justifying or if you're just exaggerating." Catherine said.

"Do you know Killian, the Vegetables Seller?" Francis asked Catherine.

"Yeah, the one that sells vegetables in the village centre." Catherine replied.

"He also sells vegetables on his motorcycle in the streets of Ferrierfield.
But, have you ever seen him sell anything to anyone in our street or at least even pass by our street?" Francis said.

"No. You go to his shop and get them from there." Catherine answered.

"And have you ever seen him walking perfectly with his two legs?" Francis asked.

"No, he drags one of his legs." Catherine replied.

"Yeah, it must have made sense to you, at least now." Francis said.

"Francis, what are you even trying to say?" Catherine asked.

"Killian and Elsie were classmates. When they were around fourteen, Elsie used to be the Class Coordinator. She got that role out of the respect that her class teacher had for my father. Later, the same class teacher replaced her with Killian as the class coordinator after noticing that her grades were getting worse day by day.
Killian studied well and was also a bit of a jerk back then.

The other reason for placing him as the coordinator is his dance performance that he did in one of the school events, for which he also won some prizes. A week later, after school, while we were coming back home, I saw her pushing him off of a height. That fall resulted in him breaking one of his legs. And that's the same leg that you'll see him dragging today." Francis said.

"I know that she is a bad person. But what you might have seen can also be an accident, right?" Catherine said.

"It's her deliberate action. After pushing him, she screamed, 'Dance Nowww, you jerk'."

"From that day-
He never danced,
He never came to school &
He never even dared to pass through our street.
And that's the real Elsie that you people never got to see." Francis said.

Catherine felt terrified. She sat silent, not knowing how to respond to Francis's words.

"And you might say that it's just an immature and unintentional act of hers. I witnessed another incident three days ago." Francis said.

"What happened?" Catherine asked.

"A few days ago, Monika created a scene, and it got serious. The Police handled it at last. After that issue happened, Charles called me and spoke with me in person.

He asked me to monitor Monika for a few days to see if she's still meeting the guy that's said to be her boyfriend." Francis said.

"Elsie deserves such a child. Instead of minding her business, she pokes her nose in everyone else's house. At least now she'll be busy handling her daughter's mess." Catherine said.

"One day, she took Monika to Tacro for shopping. Monika's boyfriend came there. From the way he walked and spoke, it was evident that he was drunk. While they were leaving the store, he started following them. I wanted to wait for some more time and go help them if needed.
They tried avoiding him first. But, when he kept coming after them, Elsie took a rock and hit him in the head without even thinking about how hard and where it would hit him. It hit him partly in the eye and he started bleeding. When he fell on the ground, she started screaming at him madly and slapped him with one of her sandals. She didn't leave until Monika dragged her from there. She didn't change even a bit. The same uncontrolled madness." Francis said.

"Let it be madness or anything else, Francis. I will not tolerate anyone laying hands on my child, no matter whoever it is." Catherine said.

"Reacting to an incident just happens in seconds, Cathie. But, if that person is harmful, the consequences will have a painful impact on us. So, try avoiding locking horns with Elsie as much as possible.
If, in some cases, the situation demands you to act against

her, do it. We can handle that then." Francis said by taking Seth near him and consoling him to sleep in his lap.

• • •

53

CHAPTER XIII

The Help

One evening, while Donovan was working in the field, Sir Charles and Jack sat on a bench under the shade of a tree.

"Sir, I didn't understand one thing." Jack said to Charles.

"What is it, kid?" Charles asked.

"You know Byron, right?" Jack said.

"Yeah, what about him?" Charles said.

"When I was a child, I used to hate it when he visited our home and sat for hours and hours discussing everything and about everyone present in our village." Jack said.

Charles laughed and said, "Why did you feel so?"

"I don't like his sheepish smile. His words don't seem genuine." Jack said.

Charles just laughed in reply to Jack's words.

"Yesterday, when I was heading towards our fields with dad, he saw us and gave a serious look, as if we had done something wrong. My dad didn't notice that. I didn't understand the meaning of the way he looked at us." Jack said.

"Recently, an incident took place. And that incident changed the atmosphere between me and him quite a lot." Charles said.

"What happened, Sir?" Jack asked.

"Do you know Wilbur?" Charles asked.

"Yes Sir, one of our neighbouring farmers." Jack replied.

"Two months ago, he came to me and discussed with me regarding the process of availing agricultural loan. I explained to him the entire process.
Byron came from a simple family. No big background. They lived in rental houses till he turned young. A man's need for money and greed makes him find loopholes present in a system, in order to benefit from it. Byron did the same. A decade ago, the villagers knew little about agricultural loans. The benefit in agricultural loans is that, Banks offer loans to farmers based on the land they had, for less interest. Back in those days, most farmers used to borrow money from the rich and ended up giving away their agricultural land and sometimes even their household land to those that lent them the money, which is clearly an injustice since the rich that lent these poor farmers the money used to charge high interest and sometimes, they used to manipulate the loan amount numbers in the bond paper.
I've heard that Byron's uncle left this village in the same way, by selling his house and household land to the village head back then, unable to repay the money that he borrowed. It hit Byron hard."

Byron isn't educated. But he managed to understand how this whole agricultural loan process works. From then, he used to help small farmers avail loans under this agricultural loan scheme. He used to charge them some money in return for his help throughout that process. He even used to cheat those farmers by misinforming them about the interest rates. Thereby obtaining all the amount procured through that extra false interest rate.

By the time he got married, he didn't have a house or land of his own. But today, he owns four acres of land and also a house here. How do you think that he has got all those by just roaming in the streets of Ferrierfield?

When Wilbur discussed with me about the loan availing process, he also mentioned that Byron is involved in it. Byron initially approached Wilbur with the loan proposal. Wilbur trusts me, and hence he came for my help, to avail the full amount of loan without letting any greedy hand's involvement in it. I've known Wilbur for a long time. He minds his own work both in the field and in the village. That man has children to feed. He earned the bare minimum from his crops. So I decided to help him with the loan process, even if it meant going against Byron.

Three fourth of our villagers are the spies of rich and other influential people like Byron. So, Wilbur used to meet me at our house after sunset. I have clearly explained to him the entire process and also arranged all the required documents. One fine day, Wilbur went to the Bank in Tacro, hoping that he'd get the loan. But, he came back hopelessly saying that the concerned loan officer is asking him to bring some other missing documents, which sounded like he's intentionally delaying the process. The next day, I visited the Bank along with Wilbur and told the officer that I'm aware of the entire loan process. I clarified that Wilbur is financially weak and hence cannot afford to take the help of agents such as Byron. That officer knew that I'm educated. He sensed that I might complain or go to any extent against him to help Wilbur. Thus, Wilbur was granted the loan without the need to pay Byron even a single lever (Crancktonian Currency).

From that very next day, Byron neither stepped into our premises nor smiled like the old times, on seeing me." Charles said.

Jack has a huge respect for Charles. After knowing this, his respect for Charles has raised a bar more.

• • •

CHAPTER XIV

Letter for Jack

One morning, while Charles and Donovan were casually discussing the yield of that year, the postman arrived and handed over Donovan an envelope addressed to Jack. On seeing the 'from address', Donovan said that it's from the college. Thinking that they might be the scorecards, Charles took it from Donovan, opened it and found that it's a letter for Jack from the college management.

Donovan observed an immediate change in Charles's facial expressions after reading that letter.

"What's wrong?" Donovan asked Charles.

"What's he doing?" Charles asked Donovan about Jack.

"He might have got up by now. Probably having his breakfast." Donovan replied.

"Ask him to meet me when he's done with having breakfast." Charles said.

Donovan went to his house and informed Jack that Charles had called him. Janet served them breakfast. Then Donovan went to Charles's, followed by Jack.

"I thought you were here on holidays!" Charles announced when Jack arrived.

"What happened, Sir?" Jack asked.

"Here's the letter for you. Sent by your college management regarding your suspension. They sent this to inform you to return to the college by the 28th of next month." Charles said.

Donovan failed to understand whether what he's witnessing right at that moment is really happening or if it's his dream.

"Can you explain to us why you hid this from us?" Charles asked.

The Bullies:

Back in the month of March, Jack went out in search of an internship for two weeks. He didn't find any and hence returned to the college. On the day of his return, he didn't find his Best Friend Calvin in the class. Jack thought that Calvin might have called sick.

After the college, Jack immediately went to the hostel where Calvin stays and found him in the corridor. While he was standing near his room with just a towel around him, Jack asked Calvin, "Coming from the shower?"

"My roommate locked the room and went to the college. I have been waiting here like this since this morning." Calvin replied in an exhausted tone.

"What happened to your pair of keys?" Jack asked.

"I don't carry them to the shower and my roommate is aware of that. I don't know why he did this." Calvin said.

Ten minutes later, Calvin's roommate returned playfully laughing and chit-chatting with his friends. Jack observed an unusual smirk on his face.

On seeing Calvin, his roommate exclaimed, "Calvin! What are you doing in the corridor? Didn't you come to college?"

"Why did you lock the room when you knew that he went for the shower?" Jack asked it straight on his face.

"The warden came in the morning on his rounds. He instructed us to lock the rooms. So, I locked it up and rushed to the college. I forgot about Calvin." the roommate said.

"Strange! The warden is a nice guy. Anyway, open it up." Jack said.

Upon checking his bag, he said, "Oh! I forgot them in my friend's bag. Wait, I'll get them."

A few minutes later, he returned with the keys.

"I'm starving. Can you accompany me to the canteen?" Calvin asked Jack while getting dressed up.

"Yeah. Even I'm feeling hungry. Didn't eat properly during the lunch hour." Jack said.

Having seen them leaving for the canteen, Calvin's roommate asked him to bring him something for dinner.

After having a satisfactory meal, on seeing Calvin heading towards the Parcel Section, Jack asked him, "You ate half of the canteen's production already. Still feeling hungry?"

"Hahha, no. Need to get the food parcel for my roommate." Calvin said.

"Today you aren't gonna do any service to him. I won't let you." Jack said.

"Why so?" Calvin asked.

"In the evening, I observed a smirk on his face. Moreover, I found no concern on his face. Victor lives in your adjacent room and he came late to the class this morning. How come does the Warden leave him?
Seems like, that clown is trying to fool us around." Jack replied.

"Maybe you're right, but what might he have against me?" Calvin said.

"We are about to find it. Let's prepare the cheese in order to lure the rat out.
As a part of our cheese preparation, let's roam here until it gets dark. Most importantly, keep those peace philosophies

of yours to yourself and do as I say." Jack said.

"Sure, Your Honour." Calvin replied, laughing.

They roamed in the empty ground for around two hours discussing the movies, family matters and everything that came to their mind.

"When we reach your room, pass me your set of keys and be late to the shower from tomorrow. Continue being late to the shower until your roommate locks you out like he did today." Jack said.

Calvin nodded as a sign of acceptance.

They returned to Calvin's room by 8:30 PM. As agreed, Calvin secretly passed his set of keys to Jack. For a continuous five minutes, Calvin's roommate showed off as if he was reading something seriously while repeatedly throwing looks at Calvin, expecting the dinner parcel. Having observed Jack & Calvin chit-chatting, he asked them about his dinner parcel.

"Oh! We totally forgot about that. How did we even forget that Calvin?
Seems like the forgetfulness has possessed pretty much everyone here." Jack said in a dramatic tone.

On hearing that, Calvin's roommate immediately jumped out of his bed, took his plate and ran towards the hostel canteen.

The very next day, Calvin went late to the shower and was locked out like the day before. Jack arrived with Calvin's set of keys and they left for college after Calvin got dressed up.

By the time they reached the college, Calvin's roommate was seen handing over the keys to a guy standing in a group of three. "Here we go again. I locked the room just like yesterday. He won't be coming today too." Calvin's roommate told them with a sheepish smile. The shortest one among the three slapped Calvin's roommate and said, "What did we tell you? To repeat nothing, right? Are you out of your mind?". "Damn, here they are. How did he even come here if you really locked him out of the room? Are you trying to play us?" the tall one of them said, looking at Calvin and Jack.

Jack & Calvin didn't hear them though, but they clearly observed the sign of disagreement between the three and Calvin's roommate. The three guys left hurriedly, acting as if they hadn't noticed anything.

"Now I understand why he's doing what he's been doing for the past few weeks." Calvin said.

"Why does it take you so long to realise when something is wrong, Calvin?" Jack said.

"Patience, Jack." Calvin said while he kept looking straight at his roommate and those three guys that were leaving from there.

"So, tell me, what's the matter?" Jack questioned while aligning his look at Calvin's roommate with Calvin. They kept staring at him until he ran away from there.

"Chris has been friendly with me for the past few weeks. That trio didn't like it. That's pretty much it." Calvin answered.

"Why is she being friendly with you all of a sudden? That too when I was away from college?" Jack said, out of suspicion.

"Maybe you're acting as a woman-guard for me." Calvin said, laughing.

"Did she actually say that?" Jack asked.

"Not exactly. But she partly said it." Calvin said, laughing.

"Clearly this is so much of an exaggeration, kid." Jack said smiling.

After college, Calvin's roommate arrived one hour late to the hostel and unlocked the door only after verifying that it's locked from the outside. He was shocked to find Calvin and Jack waiting in the room just for him to come. Although he tried to run away from there, Calvin caught him and Jack locked the door. Jack thrashed him multiple times to get the truth out of him. He gave it out easily. Those three guys that you saw this morning didn't enjoy seeing Chris moving closely with Calvin and hence they decided to trouble him.

"What are you guys arguing about in the morning when we arrived there?" Jack asked.

"They asked me to never repeat their plans in order to avoid suspicion. They burst at me with anger for locking Calvin for the second day straight." Calvin's roommate said.

"So, why did you lock him out today?" Jack asked.

"You two didn't bring me food from the Canteen yesterday & because of that, I ate that tasteless food in the hostel canteen. So, I locked him up again." he replied.

Jack slapped him and said, "If you ever dare to do something like this to my friend or anyone else again, don't forget that I'll be there to teach you a lesson."

Two days later, Jack, Calvin and a few of his friends that are staying in the hostel were late to the first hour (class). The subject of first class on that day is "Interpretation of Statutes". It is taught by an Assistant Professor popularly known by the nickname "Caveman" which perfectly justifies his actions. He grew more serious and started behaving abnormally after his divorce.

Having observed the irritation on Jack's face, Calvin whispered, "Our Caveman is really a punctual & extraordinary person, isn't it? Wherever he is, he wants his students to stand out from the group."

"Yeah, he made us stand out by making us stand outside the class. And here you are, probably the one and only about to be extinct cum devoting student follower of him, representing his excellence."

Caveman borrowed the following class too in order to finish the pending modules of the syllabus on time. He didn't allow those that were standing outside, even in the second hour, into the classroom. Finally, Jack and Calvin got the chance to sit in the third hour. They were so tired that they didn't even eat breakfast. In the lunch hour, it took them twenty minutes to reach the college canteen, which will usually be less than ten minutes walk. They moved like tortoises with hungry stomachs. Finally, they arrived at their regular spot, where they eat and spend time talking with each other in their free time.

"What the hell! Will all those that are waiting in the queue get to eat this afternoon?" Jack said out loud.

"Cool down. I'll go & get something for us to eat. You aren't good with the queues anyway." Calvin said smiling, in order to cheer up Jack.

Calvin managed to get two plates of hot and freshly prepared lunch. While he was on his way back to Jack, the trio were present there. Jack saw them but ignored their presence. His hunger made him concentrate only on the food. The tall one among the trio intentionally put one of his legs in Calvin's way. Since the food on the plates was so hot and the whole place crowded, Calvin partially fell off. During the fall, he placed one of those plates on the adjacent bench. The food present on the second plate fell on his right palm and right leg and it hurt him since it was so hot.

By the time Calvin cleared the food that fell on his leg, Jack lifted him up by his hand and knocked down the one responsible for Calvin's fall with a heavy blow. The other two from the trio immediately jumped in front of Jack to fight with him. The trio doesn't have much of a good impression among the peers. Some of Jack's supporters and some that hate the trio helped Jack in fighting them off. Both the groups got injured. The fight ended abruptly after a few heavy muscles separated the two groups.

"Let's eat now." Jack said, making an impatient face.

"You should have let it go, Jack. They aren't nice people. And they aren't thinking with their brains." Calvin said while observing the wounds on Jack's face.

"To hell with these bullies. This ain't the place for bullying and I ain't the person that entertains this kind of behaviour." Jack said.

They both shared the single plate of food that survived the fall. After lunch, Calvin accompanied Jack to the Medication Centre. By the time Jack & the trio that were involved in the fight got back to the classroom, the Principal already summoned them. Jack was already prepared for the consequences right at the moment that he lost his temper. But all he was worried about was Calvin. He doesn't like that fight to affect Calvin. All he wanted was to see Calvin in a safe and peaceful environment.

The Principal clearly hated to see blood on his campus grounds. A heated discussion took place in his office where he threatened everyone involved in the fight with the word

"Detention". The trio has already faced detention thrice in the past for some mischievous acts.

"I thought that you both are good students. What made you get involved in this fight?" The Principal said, pointing at Jack and Calvin.

"These guys have been causing us inconvenience for a lot of days, Sir. And I reacted to it today." Jack said.

"Do you know that there is an administration over here, to which you can complain against them about their activities? They're rogues anyway. This isn't the first time that they're standing guilty in my office. But what's wrong with you? I feel ashamed to say that you are Law students from my college. Those that have studied here are in prominent positions in the society at present." The Principal said.

"Sir, this morning we were made to stand outside the class for a continuous two hours for being late to the class. Our energy levels almost drained up by the time we reached the canteen. And I think you are aware of the usual length of the queue that can be observed at the canteen, especially during lunch. Neither that queue decreases nor the lunch time increases. It is the same time that they chose to trouble us." Jack answered.

"Why were you late for class?" The Principal asked.

"Water Issue, Sir." Jack answered.

The Principal then spoke with the hostel warden on phone and verified the truth in Jack's allegation. With no other thought, he immediately dismissed the trio by informing them that they're suspended for six months. Then he spoke personally with Jack and Calvin.

"See guys, I have nothing against you two. I understand that certain situations made you stand guilty in my office today. But, for being involved in the fight within the campus, I must suspend you two too." The Principal said with a hopeless expression.

"Sir, I very well understand that you must take some action against me. But Calvin is the victim of this whole incident. He never retaliated. So, can you please not include him in the suspension?" Jack said.

The Principal thought about it and surprisingly agreed. Jack got suspended for three months.

• • •

All these incidents flashed before Jack's eyes when Charles asked him, "Can you explain to us why you hid this from us?" by looking at the letter sent by the college management. And it took him a minute to process all these and reply to Charles's question.

"I have a Best Friend named Calvin in college, Sir. I got into a fight with three guys that bullied him and troubled him for a long time. The fight got bigger when their and our supporters with different agendas entered the fight. The bullies got suspended for six months and I got suspended for three months."

The word "Bullies" hit Charles differently. While Jack was prepared to answer what he did during his first one and half months of suspension, Charles got lost in thought and said, "You can leave, Jack." Everyone over there felt surprised that Charles left Jack without giving any lecture.

• • •

CHAPTER XV

The Enduring Pain

15.1 The Enduring Pain: In the Smiling Heart

That afternoon, Donovan didn't take a chance to question or point out Jack for what he did, for he himself felt that he too might have reacted in the same or more aggressive manner. But Janet failed to keep calm. She annoyed Jack by telling him that he should have stayed calm instead of reacting to those bullies. Before Jack reacted to her words, Donovan told her to stop discussing that and carry on with her work. She then left from there murmuring something.

Charles came knocking on Donovan's door in the evening and asked for Jack. He asked Donovan to inform Jack to come to the Farm if he's free. Having heard Charles's words, Jack woke up from his quick nap and washed his face. By the time he came out of the house, Charles was waiting on his porch just for Jack. The Farm is three kilometres away from their house. Jack & Charles left for the Farm on the motorcycle.

"Let's sit there on the bench and talk." Charles said.

"Sir, are you upset about my suspension?" Jack asked while walking towards the bench.

"No, Jack." Charles replied, thinking about something else.

Charles let out a deep breath and continued, "Situations and people are strange, Jack. They make us feel, fight and forget. They make us feel something for someone or for ourselves. They make us fight with other situations or people. And they make us forget who we are and what we are doing at that moment.

Sometimes, something that's Morally correct is Ethically incorrect. But that shouldn't stop you from fighting for what needs your presence and support. The way you chose to fight against those bullies is against the principles of that land. If you do the same outside your campus and no one sees it, it's a fair play. But, also, you must be aware that the Police or other authorities monitor the outside world. So, no matter wherever you are present, there'll be someone that'll stop you from doing what you're trying to do to serve justice to someone. So, fight it, but choose your ground wisely.

Most importantly, remember one thing Jack, you'll only be strong enough and authoritative enough to fight for justice when you're a youngster and later when you become an adult. After crossing those stages, you'll mostly hesitate to make a move. There'll be several things that'll stop you from doing what you want to do at that time. And you can earn respect and trust earlier and make use of them later on."

"Okay Sir. Honestly, it's a lot to process right now. But thank you for explaining all this." Jack replied.

"Take your time Jack. And I didn't ask you to come here to tell you all these philosophies. There's something else that I want to share with you." Charles said.

"What is it, Sir?" Jack asked.

"Did your father ever tell you about my elder brother?" Charles questioned.

"Yes, Sir. I remember him telling me that your elder brother ran away from home at a young age and never returned." Jack answered.

"Yeah, my elder brother, William, was the obedient one among all our siblings. He is so sensitive that he used to get hurt easily and even cry for little things. No matter what time of day or night it was, he would help our father in the field. He almost never skipped school. I learned a lot from him.

My parents treated all our siblings the same. William had dark skin while the rest of us had a light brownish one. When he was at school, he was bullied for his colour. Sometimes he used to complain about it at home, but none of us took it much seriously.

One day, he didn't come back home after school. We thought that he might have gone to the farm directly after school in order to help our father. That evening, our father came home from the farm by 6 o'clock. When asked about William, he said that he didn't come to the Farm. My father and I then went to his schoolteacher's house and found out that he left school at lunch hour saying that he is not feeling well. Till then, my father stood strong, hoping that he might have gone to his friends to play with them. But when his teacher told us that he left in the afternoon saying that he was not feeling well, it literally shook my father. Then he remembered William complaining about the bullies at school. He asked me to go to their houses and ask them if they teased him earlier that day. When I went to the houses of those bullies and told them that William went missing, each one of them denied bullying him but blamed the other members of their group of teasing him about his colour by saying that he does not belong to our family and he might be adopted. Although some of them denied bullying him and some blamed others in their group for bullying him, it was evident that he got bullied by those people that day at school.

By the time I approached my father to inform him that he was bullied that day at school, he was making some boatmen search for William in the huge pond present near the school. I was literally crying when the boatmen were searching for his body in the pond. My father and I felt a bit better when the boatmen found nothing in that pond. When we reached home, my neighbours were sitting around my mother trying to console her while she kept weeping out of pain. My younger brothers sat beside my mother in a terrified and confused state. My parents ate nothing that night. I fed my younger brothers, for they sat silently without asking for food even when they're feeling hungry. That night, I kept praying to all the gods to send my brother back home. That's the first and last night that I prayed to god. It took my parents a month to accept and move on with his absence.

It's been almost more than forty years that he ran away from home and all of our lives. But I still cannot forget the way I prayed and wished for his return. That wound stayed fresh within me. After a lot of years, today, I heard the term bullied and all the moments that I spent with him, and all the memories of him helping our family and all the memories of him taking care of us when we were little, and all the memories of the pain that settled in our hearts after he left us, have flashed before my eyes.

Your suspension has worried me when I first read about it. But, when you told me that the reason for getting suspended is because of standing against the bullies, I felt proud of you. I always think how great it would have been if my parents or I supported and took some action against those that bullied him. Every night when I get back to bed, I feel burdened to close my eyes in order to sleep, afraid of forgetting my long-lost brother's face. But, from today, after seeing my grandson save his friend from bullies, that burden will feel a little less, and I might sleep a bit peacefully."

After listening to Charles's words, tears rolled in Jack's eyes. He was out of words by the time Charles finished speaking. It took Jack almost ten minutes to control himself from crying out. He somehow managed to wipe his tears without Charles noticing it. He broke the silence by saying, "It's getting dark, sir." for which Charles replied, "Yeah, let's go home."

• • •

15.2 The Enduring Pain: In the Sweetest Hearts

That night, Jack failed to sleep peacefully after listening to Charles's pain that he has been carrying in his heart for so long. He failed to imagine his life without Richard. That morning, when Charles asked him to leave with no debate about the suspension, Jack felt lighter and thought of having a good sleep that night, for he failed to sleep well thinking about the ways to heal Stella's pain all those days. He anyway knew that, no matter how much he thinks about William, he's probably not gonna come back. But he at least wanted to help his little sister in feeling better. He got up from bed and looked at the clock while searching for his sandals to go to Stella. But, he got back to bed after noticing that the time was already 10:00 PM. Stella usually goes to bed by 08:30 PM.

The next day, after lunch, Jack went to Margaret's to see Stella. She was already sleeping by the time he went there. Margaret came out of the living room, making sure that Stella was left undisturbed. She gestured Jack to wait in the hall area when she noticed him leaving. Margaret brought him some grapes to eat.

"How are you, Aunt?" Jack asked.

"Stella is acting strange from the past few days and that's worrying me a bit at the moment. Other than that, everything is fine." Margaret said.

Jack sat silent, not knowing how to respond to her words.

"So, you stood for your friend, huh?" Margaret asked.

"Yes Aunt." Jack said with a smile.

"And, will you do the same for your family?" Margaret asked.

"Of course yes." Jack replied.

"Then what if an issue arises and your family member falls into a problem with himself/herself being the reason for that issue?" Margaret questioned.

"Aunt, the reason for standing for my friend is his innocence. His friendship with me or my relation with our family members never makes me stand for them." Jack replied.

"I'm proud of you, my boy. If this suspension thing didn't come up, I would have stayed under the impression that my nephew is the kind of youth with the hot blood that fights for his own people. Elder people of the house may say that you must act patiently, but that doesn't work every time." Margaret said, smiling.

She added, "So, where were you all these days?"

"Right at the moment that I got suspended, I decided not to come home, since there are some visible wounds on my body. The next day, I sat in my hostel room thinking about where to go. Then the peon came and asked me to meet the Principal. On my way to the Principal's Office, I thought that I was summoned to be informed to leave the hostel during my suspension. But the Principal came up with some other news." Jack said.

"And what is it?" Margaret asked.

"The Principal said- *I have never seen you before in my office for getting into a fight with someone. I enquired your lecturers and found out that you're an obedient student. And I also got to know that you're looking for an internship. I have some good news for you.*

There's a friend of mine named Robert. He's pretty much popular in the Wakefield area. He is also a close associate of the famous lawyer, Mr. Miller Anderson. I am in no position to revoke your suspension. But here is my letter of recommendation. This letter can help you get the position of an intern under Mr. Miller Anderson.

If I were you, I wouldn't miss this opportunity." Handing me over a letter of recommendation with his signature on it. I joined there as an intern and stayed with Mr. Robert for the last one and a half months.

Jack observed the fading smile on Margaret's face when he uttered the name Robert. When he observed that the smile on her face vanished completely, he asked her if she's okay.

She took a minute to come out of her deep thought and broke the silence by saying, "I'm not okay, Jack. I wasn't okay for decades. No matter how great my mood is, when I hear the name Robert, nothing can prevent me from collapsing. I might be physically smiling. But, there is a part of me that cries every single day for the person that has once left and might never come back." with tears in her eyes.

"Aunt, I'm so sorry. I didn't know that this name would hurt you and bring you back these darkest memories. If you want to talk about that, please do. We can get rid of some burden if we let out what's been bothering us for a long time." Jack said.

"All these years, I didn't hide it intentionally. The reason I kept it to myself is that- nobody in this house really seemed to be bothered about how I was feeling about my past. Even my father never made an attempt to heal my pain. All they might have seen in me is a physically smiling person.

I enjoy looking at the way you and Richard behave with each other. I love my brothers very much. In one way, I see a part of myself in you. On top of all these, you treat Stella very well. And this makes you a person that's worthy of knowing about me."

"Back in my college days, I met a person named Robert. We were classmates in the school as well. But we never interacted with each other until we entered college. Our sensitive and innocence levels matched with each other and we eventually ended up loving each other by the time we entered our final year of college.

By the time we were nearing the end of the first semester, the word about me and Robert fell in Sir Charles's ears somehow. Sir Charles didn't agree for our marriage, since Robert is from a disturbed family. Later, he agreed to it, saying that Robert must come and live with us as the son-in-law of our household, so that they need not be worried about my safety anymore. He even agreed to it.

In a very short time, Sir Charles built this house for us to live in after our marriage. On the day of marriage, Robert didn't show up. Later, we got to know that he left Ferrierfield and me. He left a letter for me that read: *I have decided to live a life of my own. I'm tired of being someone's puppet all these years, and I do not want to be that person anymore. I was hurt and I'm sorry if this hurts you. Marry a*

man that will live with you and within your heart till the end.
It took me more than a week to understand that it's no bad dream. I failed to digest the fact that the love of my life has run away from me to live a life of his own. The love that we had for each other, that's definitely not ordinary. Even till today, I'm more confused than hurt. Sir Charles shouldn't have asked him to come and live with us here after the marriage. But, he said what he said- for the sake of his daughter's well-being. Anyway, it all happened in a snap and hit me hard like a slap, whose slap marks are still there in the depths of my heart.

A month later, I decided to go out and search for Robert. Sir Charles disliked this idea. One night, with the help of some of my friends, I wrote a letter saying that I'm going out in search of Robert and to not search for me till I return on my own and left the house. I stayed at my friend's while I searched for Robert. My friend asked me to stay at her place for however long I wanted to. But she advised me that- chasing a man that has run away from the marriage isn't a good idea. Since it's about Robert, I didn't listen to her words. At that point, all I'm concerned about is finding him.

I felt exhausted after searching for him for a year and still not being able to find him. At that time, Henry's Sister was also living in that area for a while. She was working as a nurse there. One fine day, she informed me that there's a newborn whose mother lost her life while giving birth to her. She said that the relatives of that baby aren't willing to take her in and they asked the hospital authorities as well as an NGO to give her for adoption if anybody is willing to. Then I felt that my ruined relation with our family members cannot in any way be repaired. This little baby appeared like a sign of a new beginning in my life. So I adopted that sweet little girl and named her 'Stella'. Till then I was in no mood to come back to this house or these people. But, I wanted to give this little girl a family that'll treat her right and help her shine bright. Hence, I returned home with Stella a year after I left searching for Robert.

After I got back home with just days old Stella, some said that it might be Robert's child. Some said that Robert might have cheated on me. Some even said that I might have run away from home faking the search for Robert, while actually being pregnant with Robert's child. My father never cared to ask me whether it's Robert's child or not. I told Anna that Stella is an adoption. I don't believe that she believed in me that day. Your dad and Francis loved her very much right from the day I brought her here. I didn't expect Elsie to be fond of Stella and proving my expectation, she never seemed to be concerned about her and that didn't bother me though.

So this is almost everything about the phase of my life that's not so much known to you." Margaret explained.

This literally shook Jack. He failed to reply immediately, thinking that he might cry out loud in tears, which he's definitely ashamed of doing in front of someone. He is emotional, but he also makes sure that he doesn't cry in front of others. He took some time. Margaret understood Jack's trouble and went into the kitchen to bring him some water. After she passed him the water bottle silently, he emptied nearly half of the bottle. Jack cleared his throat and said sorry to Margaret.

"What are you sorry for, Jack?" Margaret asked, looking straight into his eyes.

"I know why Stella is behaving that way. I wanted to solve it. But, failed to make any move to solve her problem. I didn't know how to react after the recent issue between Aunt Elsie and Seth." Jack said.

"Does Elsie have anything to do with this?" Margaret asked.

"Speak up Jack. If I get to know what's bothering my little girl, I might be able to help her." Margaret said.

"Stella told me that, one day, while she was leaving from Aunt Elsie's, she kind of said that Stella is an orphan. And Stella took that to heart." Jack said, explaining everything that Stella told him.

Margaret let out a deep breath and said, "Psychopath! She is such a cruel person and her cruel acts don't seem to have an end."

When Margaret is done saying all this, out of the blue, Stella immediately ran into Margaret's lap, hugged her tightly and said sorry for being moody for the past few days. Stella listened to all of this by standing behind the closed door of the living room. To Jack's surprise, Margaret consoled her daughter instead of firing up against Elsie. Although she isn't a peace-preacher, she decided to respond to Elsie's action later. Jack took one of Stella's hands and kept rubbing it smoothly to calm her down.

"Look Stella, I'm not gonna lie to you. I adopted you when you were a little baby. But all I want you to understand is that- I'm not lucky enough to give birth to a wonderful girl like you. But, I'm lucky enough to find you as a gift and get the opportunity to raise you." Margaret said, holding her other hand and hugging her tight.

After a while, when Stella calmed down, Margaret told Jack with a little smile, "I'm sorry if I frightened you with my sudden tears and past."

"During my childhood, I avoided your company, thinking that you're no different from Aunt Elsie. But, in later stages, when I realised that you're the sweetest person in the family, I started coming over to your house. Like you said, your smile and sweetest way of receiving others made me think that you're happy, Aunt. Before I came here, I thought that I know my family well and I can enjoy my stay here well with my family members. But, after coming here, I'm slowly getting to know what each person in our family really is, Aunt." Jack said.

"So, tell me, what is this Robert that you met like? Is he married? Does he have children?" Margaret asked.

"All I know is that- he has a daughter that's nearly our Stella's age. When I stayed with him, she wasn't there. Mr. Robert said that she went over to her Grandma's. He doesn't have a wife or anyone else. But, Mr. Miller's family treats him really well. They're like a family."

"Ahh, I see." Margaret said.

• • •

CHAPTER XVI

The Crisis

The Story of the Maple in Sir Charles's Yard:
In 2002, Elsie gave birth to her second child. It is a boy. That baby boy suffered from high fever seven months after he was born and died of it. Her little son's sudden death badly hit Elsie. Francis then came up with the idea of planting a Remembrance Tree. Based on Elsie's choice, Sir Charles managed to acquire an Amur Maple Plant from an acquaintance.

If Elsie's son was alive, he would be of nearly Jack's age. This is also one of the reasons why she hates Jack. There were a lot of days where she silently wept and asked God why it's her child that's taken away from her and not any other child in that house.

• • •

The Present Day:
Early in the morning, Donovan went to the village centre and brought home a bag of urea to use it in the farm the other day. Having felt exhausted, he decided to take it to the farm the next day. So, he kept it under the shade of the Maple, hoping that Seth or Stella wouldn't touch it.

Elsie observed Donovan placing that Urea bag under the shade of Maple, from her kitchen's window. Her greed immediately kicked in, even when she really had no use with it. Then she went to Francis's and informed him to take some Urea from the bag placed at the Maple. When asked "Who bought it?", she told him that Donovan brought it and Sir Charles paid for it.

Francis is an opportunist. He felt that- bringing a few fists of it might come handy someday. Even before Francis reached the Maple for it, Elsie opened the bag and kept it ready for him to take how much ever he wanted from that easily. After a while, when everybody was around, Francis brought a sac with him and took nearly five kilograms of Urea in it. His ignorant behaviour has let him leave the mouth of that Urea bag opened. Later, Elsie came to the Maple making sure that no one was noticing her and took some urea into a bag and silently left from there.

The day before this whole Urea drama took place, Donovan observed Charles giving money to Frederick, which Frederick later used to drink alcohol. So he went to Charles, asking for a temporary debt. Charles told him that he has got no money left to give him. Then Donovan kind of got irritated with this and borrowed that money from one of his friends. Elsie witnessed Donovan asking Charles for money. She went to Francis and told him that Charles paid for it, in one way to escape from her theft if Donovan doesn't react to Francis's act and in another way to spark a fight between her two brothers.

In the afternoon, while almost everyone is sleeping, Seth found the Urea bag while playing in the open area near the Maple. He playfully kept hitting that bag as if it was a punching bag. Since the bag is tightly packed, he hurt his hand a bit, and it angered him. Then he kicked it hard with his foot as if he was practising karate and that bag fell off, resulting in the chemical falling at the base of the trunk. The chemical that fell over there is way too excess even if it is spread among five trees.

Seth then set the bag back in its position. But he left the spilled chemical untouched, for his nose and eyes started feeling irritated by its smell. He then observed the neighbouring hens wandering in their yard. He intentionally shooed them towards the Maple so that they'll dig up the soil around the base of the trunk which will result in the Urea going down the topmost layer of the soil. Later in the evening, Stella came there and noticed that no one had watered the plants in almost a week or so. So she watered all the trees and plants there. She usually has the habit of watering more to the trees, for she feels their thirst.

The next morning, Donovan went to the Maple and found that the mouth of the Urea bag was open. After examining it, he understood that one fourth of the chemical had gone missing in just one day. He came back to his house and asked Janet if she knew anything about the Urea that had gone missing from the bag that he had placed under the shade of the Maple the day before. Janet told him that she has seen Francis take some of it into a sac. Donovan then went straight to Francis's and asked him if he had some Urea. Francis told him that he hadn't any. Donovan then demanded him to get that from somewhere. This led to a heated argument between the two brothers. It resulted in Francis throwing the sac of Urea in front of Donovan, which nearly missed hitting him, that he brought from the actual bag the day before. Thus, a verbal fight started between the two brothers. Then Francis accused

Donovan of taking money from Charles to buy that bag of Urea and said that it makes him eligible to take the quantity of Urea he wants. Donovan then brought Charles there and asked him if he had given him any money. Charles said that he hasn't given any money to Donovan. Francis continued quarrelling despite being present in a confused state.

Margaret tried stopping them but failed to do so. Letting her two brothers fight for a straight fifteen minutes, Elsie entered the scene slowly and stood there as if she had nothing to do with that fight.

On noticing Elsie's arrival, Francis said, "Elsie, come, why did you tell me that Charles gave money for the Urea Bag bought by Donovan?"

In a melodramatic tone, Elsie said, "I think, you haven't heard me clearly, Francis. I didn't tell you that Sir Charles gave him any money. I just informed you to get some Urea from that bag present under the Maple by asking Donovan's permission." Pointing her index finger at the Maple.

She noticed that something was wrong with the Maple. She then turned in the Maple's direction and found that the Maple had dried up completely and died. She was recollecting her previous day's memory where the Maple was fine when she saw it while Donovan was placing the Urea bag under its shade.

Elsie immediately ran towards the Maple crying, "Oh! My Son! What happened to you? Who did this to you?" She screamed and cried out in pain. Charles examined the Maple's trunk base and announced that the Maple had died because of the Fertiliser Burn. Thinking no further, she blamed Donovan, saying that he's the one that's behind this. In reply to her words, Donovan said that he has nothing to do with that. Janet said that Donovan had gone nowhere near the Maple the day before, after dropping that bag there.

The entire family stood there while Elsie collapsed on the ground and kept weeping. Frederick said that he saw Stella watering the Maple for about twenty minutes the previous day. Elsie failed to control her anger and tried reaching for Stella's hair to pull her down onto the ground. Even before she reached Stella's hair, Margaret reached out to Elsie's hair in just a fraction of a few milliseconds, got a tight grip of it and pulled her back suddenly, which shocked everyone present there. It hurt Elsie badly. Even Elsie was shocked to see Margaret react in such a way, so she kept looking at Margaret's face with a hollow expression.

Margaret said, "Feel happy for getting pulled back by my stimuli. If you dare lay your hands on my daughter, you will not even be able to crawl back to your living room which is just a few feet away from here, for I will break anything and everything that supports your movement from the spot that you're lying in now. Then you'll be left with our beloved father and your drunkard husband to carry you from here."

Elsie understood that Margaret's rage had crossed its boundaries already and said, "If you were me, if this tree was a memory of your dead son, would you remain calm?" in order to make Margaret fall into a state of dilemma.

Margaret immediately responded to her words by questioning Stella whether she watered the Maple tree the previous day and also why she did so. Stella said in a terrified tone that she usually waters that tree thrice a week. She also said that she found the Maple tree in a dry state after she didn't step out of the house for a week. She concluded by saying that those are the reasons that made her spend almost twenty minutes watering the Maple and the other plants as well, the previous day.

With a fixed serious look on Elsie, Margaret said, "Look Elsie, if it wasn't for the respect that I had for our father, I would have chased you out of this place long ago. You might be the firstborn of this house, but that won't make you any greater than any of our brothers. Expecting care and love from others is okay, but the selfishness that you have to have everything for yourself is something that's not at all okay.

I might have let you punish my child even without listening to my child's version of the incident, if you were a great parent. But everybody over here is well aware of the fact that your parenting is a complete disaster. And the reason you wanted to punish my child is only out of rage and not out of the affection that you had for your second child. I don't think that either your drunkard husband or your reckless daughter cares about whether you are hurt or not, for they kept complaining instead of consoling you when you were crying for this remembrance tree. At this moment, I pity you more than I hate you."

A minute after letting go of Elsie's hair, Margaret caught a tight hold of it again, hurting her and said, "What were you even thinking by speaking out that my child was adopted, that too near her? All these years, I was just patient enough to not get provoked by your stupid actions and that might have made you feel that you can go to any extent to hurt or look down upon someone. On the day that I brought Stella to this house, I myself told you all that I adopted her. Some wisest people of this house didn't even believe me, kudos to their wisdom. And I'm completely fine with it, for I do not even want to prove that to them. I didn't even want to hide this from my child. All I wanted her to have was a safe place in this family. You made me reveal it to her at the wrong time and it's okay. Now, in all of your presence, I'm telling her- *I adopted you when you were a little baby. But I want you to understand that- I'm not lucky enough to give birth to a wonderful girl like you. But I'm lucky enough to find you as a gift and get the opportunity to raise you.*"

Margaret then set Elsie's hair free, looked in Catherine's direction and asked, "Cathie, tell me, did Elsie come to your place yesterday and tell Francis anything?"

Catherine said, "Yes, Margaret. Yesterday morning, Elsie came and informed Francis to take some Urea from the bag that's placed at the Maple. When asked 'Who bought it', she said that Donovan brought it and Sir Charles paid for it. Then Francis took a sac with him and brought nearly five kilograms of Urea in it."

"If Elsie didn't do this and if Francis wanted to take it, he would've done it when no one was around. He took that in the broad daylight when he knew that everyone was there, noticing it.

I understand your temper, brother. But he is our little brother. Given the fact that you borrowed money from someone and bought it, even I would have reacted in the same way as you did. But the one that intentionally started the fight between you is lying outside your quarrel zone. This has been happening for decades and decades. At least, from now on, be careful." Margaret told Donovan.

After a few minutes of silence, everybody dispersed.

• • •

CHAPTER XVII

The Auction

The impact of the Maple's death and the quarrel that took place because of it lasted for a month on the family of Sir Charles. One morning, when Frederick was casually gossiping with a few people at the village centre, he saw Byron and greeted him.

"Hey Byron, how are you? You look pretty much busy these days? What's the matter?" Frederick asked.

"I don't have time for this now, Frederick." Byron said as he kept walking.

Frederick followed Byron and asked, "Is it a secret or what?"

"It's about a deal. I'm looking for someone that can make use of it." Byron told Frederick.

"We know each other very well, and I have several contacts in Ferrierfield and in Tacro. So why don't you tell me what that deal is?" Frederick asked Byron.

"Okay fine, listen." Byron said and explained to Frederick about the deal.

"It sounds amazing. Count me in, Byron. I'll be there on time." Frederick told Byron and left from there hurriedly.

The word about the same deal fell in the ears of Francis through one of his friends, who is a neighbour of Byron. While Donovan was coming back home from the Farm, Byron started a casual talk with him and told him too about the deal. He also added that Elsie and Frederick are already in their preparations for signing that deal.

Charles stayed back at the Farm in order to discuss the water irrigation works with other farmers. Having thought that this meeting might take much longer than he initially expected, he asked Francis to bring his lunch to the Farm.

After the conversation with Byron, Donovan came home hurriedly and informed Janet about the deal. Janet first hesitated, but later, she felt that this deal will help them in moving away from Ferrierfield and enjoy a happy life in Tacro.

The Deal:
There are some plots in Tacro, in which some buildings are being newly built. According to the information provided by Byron, a government officer has bought those plots from the government through a bidding process and acquired three quarters of a perfect square shaped area. He is also said to have the clearance papers for the construction of household buildings in that land. Having calculated the land value and the building value in Ferrierfield, if Frederick or Elsie, Donovan and Francis sell their current old houses and give that land (on which their buildings are currently standing) for lease, they'll be receiving a good amount of money that'll be helpful for them in paying three fourth amount of the money required for buying the land present in Tacro along with the under construction buildings

standing on that land. In addition to that, the building materials needed to finish the construction of those buildings are also said to be inclusive of the deal, which means- they need not pay or spend any additional money in finishing their construction, for the owner of it has already bought them. The remaining one quarter amount of money can be cleared using the money obtained through the lease amount for their lands in Ferrierfield.

The seller of these lands (the government officer) is said to have received a government project that requires him to supervise and get some construction work done in Ferrierfield or in any other neighbouring villages with about fifteen skilled and high paid men. So, that government officer is looking to get the household land for lease and temporarily buy the buildings (to avoid the rental costs of the buildings) in them to get rid of the high level initial investments. And he is showing much interest in bringing that project to Ferrierfield.

When Francis asked Byron, "The land values in Tacro will be higher than that of Ferrierfield, then how will this whole leasing the land and selling the buildings equation work?" Byron said that the plots that are currently kept for sale are present on the outskirts of Tacro and not in the centre. This clarified the doubts of the three siblings and Frederick. The three couples (Frederick-Elsie, Donovan-Janet and Francis-Catherine) made their individual calculations and decided to make that deal. Two factors that motivated them in going for this deal. One is, they got fed up with living together unhappily. The other factor is that- the land prices in Tacro will only go up and not gonna come down. Francis sent Charles's lunch with Seth. Then Frederick and Elsie, Donovan, Francis left for The Auction Venue.

When Donovan and Francis arrived at The Auction Venue individually with their documents, Elsie came after them with some documents in her hand. For a second, Donovan and Francis didn't understand what those documents were. They thought that those documents might be of Frederick's house that's present in his hometown, which is also rumoured to be sold off a long time ago in order to clear off his debts.

The three siblings sat in different rows, apart from each other, as if they did not know each other. A few neighbouring villagers also attended the auction. Having observed the number of people coming to the event, the three siblings thought that it would not be an easy deal. Yet, they wanted to give it a try, for it resembled to them as their freedom-grabbing opportunity. While the auction is going on in a slow pace, Byron approached the three siblings individually and whispered in their ears that they can win the auction if they are willing to pay a little amount of money to the owner himself to let him help them win the auction. When they said that they didn't carry any money with them, Byron advised them to take money from him and sign on a bond paper, which can be destroyed when they repay that money. After they agreed and signed on Byron's bond papers, Byron sighed to the auctioneer to pass the result in favour of the three siblings. In just a matter of minutes, the three siblings won the auction. The others that took part in it left with disappointed faces.

They returned home happily, hoping that it would surprise their father. Instead, he was shocked by their act. Monika felt happy for her parents' win. Janet felt happy for her husband's win. And Catherine felt happy for her husband's win. Sir Charles was unusually worried about what they did, for it made him feel that something was wrong. Margaret didn't like this total moving away idea of her siblings. She is concerned about her two brothers. During the dinner that night, when Stella asked her if Donovan and Francis's families will leave from Ferrierfield for real, she wasn't ready with an answer at that moment. But, if that situation really comes, she wanted to stop her brothers from leaving.

The next day, Sir Charles asked his three children to show him their newly bought property. They asked Byron to come there, but he told them that he won't be available all throughout the day since he must go and visit one of his relatives who is present on his deathbed. So, with the help of Byron's directions over the phone, they took Charles to the place and stood there proudly, as if they had conquered a kingdom. After a thorough examination, Sir Charles announced that the under construction buildings don't seem like household buildings. He said that they are looking more like office buildings. Then he spoke over the phone with one of his close acquaintances and hung up, disappointed.

"What's wrong with you people? Are you out of your mind?" Sir Charles said.

"What happened Sir?" Francis asked.

"I just spoke with one of my old friends who has been living in Tacro for decades. He said that this land belongs to the government."

"What you just said is partly true, father. This land is previously owned by the government. A government officer has recently bought this land through a bidding process." Elsie said, explaining all the other details about the deal.

"This doesn't seem right. Come with me." Charles said and took them to Tacro's Police Station.

Then he took them straight to Officer Henry and explained to him the whole situation. Henry asked them to sit in the waiting area. He then started checking some old records and made some calls to the people belonging to different departments. Half an hour later, he came to Sir Charles and informed him that the auction in which his three children had taken part was a scam. Elsie, Frederick, Donovan and Francis were stunned at hearing Henry's words. Henry advised Sir Charles to not lodge a complaint immediately, for it'll get public as soon as they register a complaint. Henry promised Charles that he'll look into it and do everything in his power to help them. When they left the station, Henry informed Robert about all of this.

The moment the scapegoats of the auction realised that The Auction is a scam, they tried reaching Byron on the phone. He intentionally left their calls unanswered. While on the way back home, there was utter silence between Sir Charles and the victims of the scam. That night, the youngest one of Charles's brothers casually called him over the phone. Sir Charles narrated to him all about the auction and everything that happened after that event. His younger brother told him that they (he and the other brothers) will come to Ferrierfield the following day.

• • •

CHAPTER XVIII

The Reasons and The Consequences

The following day, early in the morning, two men arrived at Sir Charles and examined the overall yard where Charles and his children live with their families. When Charles asked them about their purpose of visit, they said that they're from the government, who are asked to survey the recent land and building donation by the donors named Elsie, Donovan and Francis. It is only then that Charles and his children understood the real cruel motive behind Byron's auction plan. The government officials that came for the survey handed over Sir Charles some papers which said that the donated property must be vacated in two days or less, for they'll be slightly renovated and announced by The Mayor publicly as the first biggest ever donation from Ferrierfield for the poor.

Charles' brothers arrived when the government officials were just leaving. Having thought that this issue might take a few weeks to get resolved, they arrived with bags full of clothes and some cash. Their major topic of discussion during their travel to the Ferrierfield is- how did Charles lose his house when he didn't even take part in the auction? In fact, that is the first question they asked Charles publicly (when all the family members are present there) right in the moment they saw him. Charles then revealed that he secretly transferred his house to Elsie's name after Frederick exhausted everything that they once had. Sir Charles's words made Margaret feel sad for her father. Donovan and Francis hated his over-concern on Elsie.

Anna then started blaming Elsie for being such a horrible person. When Charles's brothers tried consoling Anna, she confessed that Elsie was responsible for the death of the Maple and this whole auction mishap.

Anna said, "On the day Donovan bought that Urea Bag and placed it under the shade of the Maple, Elsie is the one that broke its seal. I saw it with my own eyes."

"Yeah, the mouth of the bag was left open by the time I reached there." Francis said.

"Why didn't you tell me this earlier?" Charles questioned Anna.

"What would we have done, even if I told you all about it at that moment? It is us that brought up our children with varied levels of affection & care. It wouldn't have gotten this worse if we treated them all equally." Anna replied.

"What is this, Mother? Are you trying to blame me and save your younger son from it?" Elsie said.

"Will you stop lying, for goodness' sake! Just do not speak anything with that foul mouth. You are such a shame to this family. It's no wonder why you are like this. You didn't inherit even a single quality from your father. You are the exact same copy of your mother." Anna said with disgust.

Among everyone that is present over there, only Sir Charles understood what Anna said. Then the youngest brother of Sir Charles asked Anna, "Why are you blaming yourself for her sins?" for which Anna kept quiet.

Then he asked Charles, "Brother, I don't understand why you pay blind-eye for everything related to Elsie? Why do you treat her so?"

"She is William's child," Charles replied in a firm tone, stuck in a deep thought.

"What!?, William's?" One of the brothers exclaimed in confusion.

"He ran away from home at the age of 14. When did you meet him?" Another asked.

"A year after I got married, I received a letter from someone named Will & I surely knew that it was him. He was living in Ferrierfield then. I rushed to his place & found that he was suffering from a disease for a long time. By that time, he has a child, and it is Elsie. He asked me to take care of his child since her mother is willing to leave after his demise, without the child. This whole yard that we are currently standing on, William used to live exactly in this place in a small hut. I bought this land from his wife, thinking that she'll then have enough money to raise Elsie. And also, I wanted to have this land as a reminder of our brother.

But, William's wife fled away from Ferrierfield with the money that she got from selling this land to me. Later I came to know that she is a nurse that used to work in the hospital that William got his treatment from. She then compelled him to marry her despite his urge that he's not gonna recover from the disease. While she sounded caring, her plans were actually the opposite. So, I brought his child to my house & brought her up as if she was my own child & the connection that I had with our elder brother, William, blinded me from seeing & acting upon her wrongdoings." Charles replied.

"Why haven't you informed any of us about this?" another brother questioned.

"I myself failed to bear the pain of his demise for a lot of years after it happened, so I decided to not give you that pain. In that moment, I felt that it is better to let you all stay in the same thought that he has left the house, never returned & was living somewhere somehow." Charles replied.

With each minute passing, Janet grew more tensed. She called Richard and Jack over the phone and informed them everything that had happened from the previous morning till the moment that she called them. She requested them to come there as soon as possible. Richard started immediately from his place. While Jack was packing his luggage hurriedly, he received a call from Mr. Robert.

"Hello Jack, are you busy?" Robert asked.

"No Sir. Please tell me what it is." Jack said.

"Is it a good time for you to come and collect the letter of recommendation that you asked for? Mr. Miller signed on it for your work as an intern under him." Robert said.

"Sir, excuse me. I don't think that I'll be able to collect it now. Is it okay for you to keep it with you for a few days, so that I can come and collect it from you soon?" Jack said.

"No worries at all, Son. I'm fine with it. But call me when you come to collect that, for I'll be out of town for a few days. In fact, I'm about to step out of my house now. By the way, I'll be passing by Ferrierfield. Do you want me to drop any of your luggage at your village? Or bring something for you from there?" Robert said.

Jack was surprised. With the closeness that he had with Mr. Robert, he asked, "Sir, would you mind dropping me at Ferrierfield? Something came up and I need to reach my home as soon as possible. It's okay if you were going somewhere on some urgent business."

Robert said, "No urgent business, Jack. It'll probably be just me and my driver. So, come over to my place. Or do you want me to pick you from your campus?"

"Thank you so much, Sir. I still need to get permission from the principal since the warden is on leave. I'll come over to your place as soon as I get the signature from the principal's office. I'm almost done with the packing anyway." Jack said in a hurried tone.

"Cool down Jack. I'll talk to the Principal if needed. Just leave from there with your luggage." Robert said and hung up the phone.

In less than five minutes, a guy came running to Jack's room and handed him the permission letter signed by the

Principal. On his way to Mr. Robert's home, Jack thought about seeking Robert's help, for he is capable of doing miracles. But he didn't dare to ask him for help, for he felt that Robert might think that Jack is asking him for too many favours.

By the time Jack reached Robert's place, he overheard Robert and Mr. Miller speaking.

"Doesn't it suffice if I go there alone?" Robert asked Mr. Miller.

"You must enjoy the luxuries when you are actually in a position to." Mr. Miller replied.

"Fine then. It seems like she needs some more time to get ready. It's already time for me to leave. So she comes in another car and the luxuries follow." Robert said.

Jack didn't quite understand what they were even talking about. While he was just smiling and physically present there, Janet's words kept repeating in his head. By the time Robert and Jack stepped out of Robert's house, a Shiny Black **H U M M E R - H2** kept roaring. As soon as they two got in, it moved smoothly with power. Robert's crew followed the Hummer, maintaining some distance.

Having thought that Robert might just be passing from Ferrierfield, Jack told him that he'll get down at the village centre. Robert nodded as a sign of okay for his words. But, he surprisingly gave his driver the directions for Sir Charles's house. Jack wondered how Robert knew all those details, for he casually mentioned that he's from

Ferrierfield in one or two conversations that they had during Jack's Internship. Donovan, Janet, Francis and Catherine were all packed and got ready to leave from their newly lost old houses when Robert and Jack just arrived there.

The roar of the Hummer caught the attention of most people present over there. While getting out, Jack wondered if this Robert is the same man that he once met in his school when an issue came up and got settled abruptly. Even before Jack invited Robert in, Robert went straight up to Sir Charles and kept looking at Margaret, who sat on the porch steps, weeping.

No one understood who this person that stood before Sir Charles was. Charles thought that this person might be an acquaintance of Jack.

"I want to speak with Margaret, Sir." Robert said.

"Do I know you?" Charles asked.

"Yes Sir." Robert replied.

"I'm sorry. I don't recognise you. May I know your name?" Charles asked.

"I'm known by the name **R O B E R T**, Sir." Robert replied.

A fleet of fifty men of Robert arrived there just then. They waited there for Robert's orders. Then Charles kept looking at the bearded Robert while trying to recollect what

Robert used to look like before he ran away from the wedding. After hearing Robert's words, Margaret slowly turned towards him and took the support of one of the porch's pillars in order to stand up. She examined him for a minute and came near him, crying loudly.

Margaret slapped Robert and said, "What made you run away that day and what made you come back today?"

Robert stood with his hands folded backwards. After Margaret slapped Robert, Jack observed Robert's left hand signalling his men to stay just where they were. If it was someone other than Margaret that has raised their hand on Robert, the environment over there would've resembled a battlefield.

"I have had my reasons for running away from our wedding that day. Either my sensitive nature or my dumbness made me run away from this place that day. But it is only later that I realised that what I did to you was wrong." Robert said with tears in his eyes.

"If you had a problem with something, you should have told me about it then and there itself. We would have sorted it out together. You left me alone and made me an orphan." Margaret said.

"It was already too late by the time I realised that what I did to you was a total injustice. Right from that moment, I kept watching you and guarding you from afar. You haven't ever seen me directly in all these years. But you were always under my constant watch." Robert said.

Margaret started crying louder, out of pain and happiness. She hugged him so tight that she wanted to get all the pain off of her chest. They felt alive again after a lot of years. Robert kept rubbing Margaret's hair in order to calm her down. She failed to control her tears even after Robert assured her that everything was going to be fine.

"I hate to see you cry. At some point of time, I was in no position to come anywhere near you and wipe your tears. But, I'm here now. I'm all yours. Tell me. What do you want me to do to make you feel happy again?" Robert said.

"I want my brothers and parents to live here with me like before. My life is already feeling empty and if they leave, I cannot live here alone in peace." Margaret requested.

"Consider it done, Darling. I'll settle everyone's scores before tomorrow evening. For the time being, can you take care of one thing for me?" Robert said.

"What is it?" Margaret questioned.

Robert sighed his sidekick to open the door of the third car in the fleet. Then a little girl stepped out of the car. Everyone was shocked to see Stella get out of that car. It made no sense to anyone over there except Robert and his men. Even Jack failed to understand how Stella got into Robert's convoy.

"Stella!" Margaret exclaimed.

When Margaret was about to say, "How and when did you get in there?" Stella interrupted her from speaking and said, "Yes Mom". Margaret got confused for a second. She clearly saw Stella getting out of the car, but Stella's voice was heard from Margaret's background. She turned her head and jumped out of surprise on finding Stella behind her, holding a glass of water.

"I just went in to drink some water, Mom." Stella said.

When Margaret turned back again, the girl that got out of the car, i.e., the lookalike of Stella, smiled at Margaret.

"What is this Robert?" Margaret questioned.

"Long story short: She is Bella. They are my Elder Sister's children. Due to some reasons, we needed to become their separate parents. I'll explain everything else later. Let me get back to the work of stopping your tears first." Robert said.

He asked Charles if he could park his cars there by the side of the road. Charles said yes. Robert then instructed his men to park their cars in a line to the side of the road in order not to cause any inconvenience to the pedestrians and other vehicles. Jack tried counting Robert's men. But he missed it somewhere in between. Fifty men came with Robert. All the fifty men and Robert went to Byron's house that night, force opened the lock, partied there and slept there for that night. Some slept in and on the top of the house, while some slept in the yard.

• • •

The Story of The Twins:

Robert had an Elder Sister. She was married to a man from the neighbouring village, who is said to be a calm going person. In reality, he acted as a calm going person when he was outside his house, to the people in the society. Behind the closed doors of his house, he behaved like a monster. He tortured his wife to an extent that he used to beat her every night that he came back from his work. She thought that he'd change sooner or later. He didn't change even a bit, even after she got pregnant. He didn't even care to think even for an instant before raising his hand on his pregnant wife.

In no time, she took the help of some council members, got her divorce from that monster, and lived in a faraway place. After a few months, she gave birth to the twins, that are now named Bella and Stella. She died while giving birth to those twins.

• • •

That night, when the clock showed nearly 12:00, Robert sat near the camp-fire made by his men in Byron's yard. As a routine, he kept thinking about Margaret, Bella, and Stella. While he was almost feeling sleepy, he noticed someone sneaking in and stood alerted with a burning log in his hand. In the light of the fire, he saw the face of the one that silently sneaked in. It was Elsie.

"It's been so many years since we last met. How are you Robert?" Elsie asked.

"Why do you care?" Robert asked.

"You are the love of my life. How can I not care for you? Maybe I'm the only person that cares the most about you." Elsie said.

"To hell with your deceitful words. Your words will not have any effect on me now. It'll just be a waste of time no matter how long you blabber. And also, I've heard that your daughter is no different from you. My Bad! Who am I even underestimating? Seems like she has perfectly inherited your traits." Robert replied.

"I thought that you'd react this way, Robert. Everything that I told you back then about Margaret and Frederick is true. I don't know how and why but, everything changed at the last minute. My father has forcefully married me to Frederick. He has been treating me worse since the first day of marriage.
I still love you. Take me from here. Let's leave this place and never return. These people aren't worth spending your time and money on." Elsie said, hoping that they'll melt Robert's heart like they did once.

Elsie left the house, making sure that everyone was asleep. But Frederick saw her leaving the room and followed her silently. He also woke up Charles and requested him to accompany him to follow Elsie to see what she's up to. After listening to what she said to Robert, Frederick failed to control his anger. He walked straight up to Elsie and slapped her thrice right in the presence of Robert and Charles and dragged her from there saying,

"Like Anna said, you are such a shame to this family of Sir Charles. I never laid my hand on you and bore every single time that you beat me, only because you're from a good family. You wanted to leave with a rich and powerful person by leaving your husband and daughter. Are you planning on carrying any money to hell after your funeral?'

"I'm sorry for misunderstanding you and Margaret all these years, Robert. I didn't raise Elsie properly, and that has affected many people. I cannot ask you for anything more than your company for Margaret, if it's possible." Charles said.

"Don't be sorry, Sir. If I were you, I would have done the same. It's only today that I understood why you treated Elsie so special. What has happened has happened and it can in no way be changed. Let's be happy for being able to see the authentic versions and reasons of people around us, at least now." Robert said.

• • •

Robert's Runaway:
A month before the wedding, Margaret got busy with the wedding preparations. At the same time, Robert was hurt with Charles's idea of asking him to be the Son-in-law of the household after the wedding. And that idea of Charles made it public that Robert's family members were not so good. He knew Elsie from the initial days of college. But they never interacted much with each other.

One day, Elsie asked Robert to meet her secretly. Robert did so.

"Margaret is trying to fool you. My father convinced her that you're not good for her. I don't know whether or not you know this, but Margaret got ready to marry a person named Frederick. You're going to be fooled in public on the day of marriage. It looks like- my father has got something against your family. He's gonna ruin all your family's name and fame on the day of the wedding by starting a fight with you in some way. It's me that has loved you right from the beginning. Even before I expressed my love to you, she approached you and grabbed you away from me." Elsie explained Robert with her fake tears.

In Margaret's absence, Elsie manipulated Robert in a way that she even kissed him once. He reciprocated it as an act of doing justice for Elsie's version of Margaret's plans. He never cared to either question Margaret if she was really planning on marrying him or confront her about everything that Elsie told him.

After Robert's runaway on the day of the wedding, some of his friends informed him that Elsie was married to Frederick. Then he enquired a few close acquaintances of Charles's family and got to know that Frederick is chosen for Elsie and not Margaret. It is only then Robert understood that Elsie destroyed the love and marriage life of Robert and Margaret. The real reason behind Elsie's fake tears and made up stories about Margaret is- Right at the moment Margaret informed Charles about her relationship with Robert, Elsie wanted to manipulate her father into declining the marriage proposal of Robert and Margaret.

In fact, it is because of Elsie that Charles asked Robert to come and live with them after the marriage, for Elsie told Charles that Robert's family isn't so nice and they might trouble Margaret after marriage. Her jealousy kicked in when Charles agreed for Margaret's marriage with Robert and grew bigger when Sir Charles started building a separate house for them. She is indeed jealous because her younger sister fell in love with such a charming and innocent man and she is getting married first. All these things led her to destroy the lives of Robert and Margaret.

By the time Robert realised that he misunderstood Margaret on listening to Elsie's words, it was already too late. He tried going back to Margaret, but the kiss that he had with Elsie made him feel that he's not as pure as Margaret. So, he decided to punish himself by keeping himself out of Margaret's house. He thought that Margaret would move on with someone in a year or two. But he underestimated Margaret's love for him.

• • •

The very same night that Robert and his men broke into Byron's house, partied and stayed there, one of Byron's neighbours who is also his supporter, has informed Byron on the phone that his house is now full of people that were partying there and breaking things. The next morning, Byron got back to Ferrierfield. Almost at the same time, Mr. Miller reached Ferrierfield to meet Robert. He first went to Sir Charles's house, hoping to find Robert there. Charles's brothers have heard a lot about Mr. Miller. They made some conversation with him and then Mr. Miller left for Byron's house.

"So they are Miller and Robert. I have heard a lot of stories about them. Most people know them for their friendship and the help they do to the people that approach them." One of Charles's brothers announced after Mr. Miller left.

Byron was shocked to find Robert at his house. It's been so long since he last saw him. Having understood that it was not an outsider that broke into his house, he relaxed his breath a bit and approached Robert with a wild laughter.

"Ah, I see, it is you. It's been so long that we last spoke with each other, Robert. You look like a completely different person." Byron said.

"Yes Byron. It's been so long that you last saw me. I'm way more different from the version of me that you knew before." Robert said.

"Yes, totally different and tough." Mr. Miller added.

"When did you come?" Robert asked Mr. Miller.

"Just a moment ago. I went to Sir Charles's house hoping that you'd be present there. They said that you stayed here last night. Was it comfortable?" Mr. Miller said.

"Yeah. We have seen worse." Robert said with a smile.

"Yeah. Seems like you are in the middle of a conversation with the mastermind behind the auction.

Carry on. I came by to see if things are going smoothly or not." Mr. Miller said.

Robert smiled on hearing those words, turned towards Byron and said, "Look, Byron, let me make it easy for you. In the process of helping someone, Sir Charles stood against you in your greedy way. You were badly hurt by that and did whatever you were capable of doing.
Enough with the display of our capabilities here. It'd be smooth and nice if you stop playing your sick games with the family members of Sir Charles and give them back their documents. Otherwise, we can settle it the other way around."

"Having seen your attire, I thought that you might have grown smart after you ran away from this place. But your words are making me feel like you are still the same immature and weak person that I last saw." Byron said with a laugh.

Robert punched Byron in his face and slapped him multiple times even before Byron realised that he was bleeding. Robert gave a pause and said, "I thought that you were wise enough to understand my words & do accordingly. But if I knew that you'd be this hot-headed, I would have told you in the only way that you would understand. I wouldn't have wasted our precious time. That too, you also need to pack your luggage to move out of Ferrierfield. So much work. Do it, waste no more time."

"Given all these men that came with you and stood with their hands folded for you here, you might have the power to harm me physically. But then I'll have other ways to defend. Like, the legal system, the police." Byron said with a smirk.

"Wow, your head is still working. Seems like you got so much skull in there and only a little brain." Robert said.

"This gentleman that is sitting over here. Do you know who he is?" Robert asked Byron, holding him by his collar, pointing at Mr. Miller.

Byron sighed that he didn't know who Mr. Miller was.

Robert said, "He's a famous lawyer named Mr. Miller Anderson. He has an excellent history or what you fancily call as the 'track record' of serving justice to the truthful people by hook or crook. And in any case, if he fails to serve justice to the victims inside the courtroom, we will make sure to break the bones of the unfavourable forces that took injustice's side."

After getting served a few more slaps and a couple of scary warnings from Robert and Miller, Byron gave up. He agreed to their terms, signed on the necessary documents, burned the bond papers and moved out of Ferrierfield. And as a result of that, Donovan and Francis got back their homes. Robert said that Byron registered Sir Charles's house in Margaret's name. Thus, Elsie got no place to live there and hence Frederick, Elsie and Monika left for Frederick's hometown.

While Robert and Mr. Miller were coming out of Byron's yard, Robert said laughing, "Have you heard what he said, Miller? He didn't know who you were. We thought that we were already famous. Seems like we need to scale up."

"As you wish, Robert." Mr. Miller replied with a smile.

After lunch, Jack went to Margaret's. Right when he entered the hall area, he found Bella and Stella playing together sitting on the couch. Jack pinched himself again (he pinched himself the previous night when Bella stepped out of the car) to make sure that he wasn't dreaming. He couldn't believe that there existed the twin of Stella in the other part of the world, that looked exactly like Stella. After noticing Jack, Stella introduced him to Bella, and they three watched TV while chit chatting in parallel till the evening. The rest of the family members too liked Bella. For Margaret, they two were an eye-feast. She just kept looking at them for hours and hours.

Mr. Miller left Ferrierfield after making sure that Robert and Margaret are happy. Then Robert went to Tacro to meet his friend Henry, a.k.a the most helpful police officer. He thanked Henry for all the help he has done in posting him every information about Margaret's well-being. In the evening, he reached back to Margaret with a heavy heart filled with mixed feelings.

"It's all done. You wasted your tears unnecessarily. Next time, just inform me what's bothering you. You are the sweetest person that I've ever met in my life and that makes you deserving of all the love and happiness present in this world. For how I did what I did to you, I thought that I'd never get an opportunity to speak with you. Thanks a lot for forgiving me." Robert said, holding Margaret's hands.

Bella and Stella stood blushing while listening to their parents' conversation.

It took Margaret a while to control her tears. With the tears in her eyes, she even failed to see Robert's face clearly. She said, "If you came here to wipe my tears, I must admit that you succeeded in doing so. Within the four walls of this house, I spent many nights weeping for you. If I knew that you'd come back to wipe my tears, I'd have cried publicly. Even now, I'm unable to control my tears associated with the pain. I want you so badly to stay here with me. So that we can enjoy our life here. Our children will grow up together and stand for each other."

"If that's really what you like, then no one can separate us from living together anymore, Darling." Robert said, hugging Margaret.

"Yes. Stay, please. We already lost so much of our together-life. Let's start this fresh." Margaret said.

The next morning, Margaret and Robert woke up next to each other, holding each other's hand and enjoying the early morning sunlight. And they lived together with love happily ever after.

CHAPTER XIX

The Little Settlement

On one occasion:
Jack fought with one of his classmates at school. The one that Jack has fought with is the only son of a village-head.

When the small fight turned into big issue, Jack felt that it might end up requiring Donovan to show up at the school.

But, a well-dressed stranger in his twenties walked up to Jack & asked, "Jack Finnigan, isn't it?"

"Yes Sir." Jack replied.

"I've heard that you're from Ferrierfield." The stranger said.

"Yes Sir, do you know it?" Jack questioned.

"Yeah, I have a few acquaintances there." The Stranger replied.

"Ohh." Jack said.

"Well, why did you fight with that kid?" Robert asked.

"He isn't behaving well with the other children, Sir." Jack said.

"& may I know why you alone wanted to respond?" The Stranger asked.

"I cannot stand injustice, Sir. To be present in such a place feels suffocating to me." Jack replied.

"Son, what you felt is right. But, there are other ways through which you can punish the ill mannered with no physical harm." The Stranger said, looking straight into Jack's eyes.

"I wonder what those ways are, Sir." Jack said.

"One of them is through Law. A lot of well-educated people (Lawyers and Judges) that has studied like you & who didn't entertain ill manners made several laws to punish the wicked. It's the best weapon & defence you can use." The Stranger said.

"That sounds great, Sir. & what's the other way?" Jack questioned.

"You'll learn it the hard way when you come of age, Son." Stranger replied & left.

Surprisingly, the stranger that discussed all these with Jack is the one that accompanied the village-head that came to take action against Jack. But that village-head left the school without even uttering a single word.

• • •

CHAPTER XX

The Way

Robert came out and sat on the sofa present on the porch. Jack stood in front of the porch, watching Stella and Bella play. On noticing Robert, Jack went and sat in the chair present against the sofa. He looked at Robert with a smile and said, "So, you're my uncle then!"

"Yes, I am." Robert said, smiling.

"There's a stranger whom I met during my schooling. I do not remember his face clearly. But his words still wander within my head. It is because of him that I chose the Law Path. Every single day of my Law Student Journey went on thanking him.

When I met you after my suspension, I wanted to ask you if you're that stranger. But, I hesitated. I want to hear it from you. Tell me Uncle." Jack said.

"Yes, Jack. I'm that stranger. I'm proud of your Law choice." Robert said.

"That Little Settlement still feels like a mystery to me. How long have we been under your watch?" Jack said.

"From a very long time. I had my special interest in you, for I saw a part of me in you. I personally feel that we react to injustice the same way." Robert said.

"It feels great to talk with like-minded people. I have a question for you?" Jack said.

"Yes, go on kid." Robert replied.

"No matter how much I try helping others, at the end of the day, I cannot sleep peacefully thinking about those that wasn't able to help. Do you feel the same?"

Robert smiled and said, "Well, I must admit that it's a good question. Listen, a lot of tragedies will happen to many people in this world while we are talking about it now,
Many people will lose their breath while we are taking our breaths now,
And it troubles me to think about all their suffering and my incapability to help them get rid of that suffering. But, also, I do not have the superpowers to help every sufferer in this world.
And I cannot stop death from taking away people from their loved ones. It hurts me to go to sleep having thought of all these. But, I avoid that pain by helping those that I can, by helping those that are around me. This is the way I chose, and this is the way that helps me keep calm despite the chaos around me."

Robert continued, "So, all I can suggest you is- Accept everything as it is and face everything in a way that you can."

"Okay Uncle." Jack said with a smile and left from there to watch Stella and Bella playing.

. . .

CHAPTER XXI

The Story of Robert

The Next Day:

"Are you feeling shy, Robert?" Margaret asked.

"Shyness and Hesitation have found their way out of me a long time ago. Why?" Robert replied.

"Back in those days, when you lived in Ferrierfield, I used to see you swim in the pond and stay bare-chested indoors. But, you haven't removed your shirt since yesterday. Are you hiding any of your other girlfriend's name or picture tattoo from me?" Margaret asked, laughing.

"Nothing like that. I just don't want to scare Stella & Bella." Robert said.

"Let me see it and say whether or not it scares them." Margaret said.

Robert locked the living room's door and took off his shirt, saying, "You have been warned."

Margaret went blank on seeing the scars present all over Robert's chest, stomach and on the back. Robert stood still till Margaret processed that image of his scars and touched those scars and said, "Is the pain still there?".

"There's no physical pain. But the reasons behind these scars are the nightmares that I can never forget." Robert said.

"Who did this to you? Why did they do this to you?" Margaret asked Robert with tears in her eyes.

"We must not weep for the cruelty of others. Always remember that. We must either fight or become better at fighting those that cause us harm." Robert said, holding Margaret's hands.

"I always wanted you to come back. That was the only thought that kept running in my mind till you returned. But I never thought about how you were doing and what you were doing. I should have searched for you for some more time. And I should have found you and stood by your side in your hard times." Margaret said, hugging Robert and feeling his scars with her smoothest palms.

"As far as I remember, you used to be chubby before you left from Ferrierfield. Now you look totally different. All those muscles and the beard. I overheard one of my uncles saying that you are quite famous on the West Side." Margaret said, helping him in putting his shirt back on.

"I cannot deny them. Time changes people. It changed me too." Robert said.

"So, may I know about you?" Margaret asked.

"Well, it's a long & kind of horror story Darling." Robert said.

"I've got a lifetime to listen & most importantly, I'm under my Robert's watch. So, tell me." Margaret replied.

To Be Continued in:

The Story of a Soul Tribe

The Story of Robert

The Story of William

• • •

Words Worth Spreading

Families are fine until they cross the line,

& when they do- you must tell them that their effort &
effect are gonna go in vain

& also make them understand that their rules & your
actions aren't entwined.

• • •

Printed by Libri Plureos GmbH in Hamburg, Germany